MERCENARY IN LOVE

J.L. ROSE
J.L. TURNER

GOOD 2 GO PUBLISHING

Mercenary In Love
Written by J.L. Rose & J.L. Turner
Cover Design: Davida Baldwin – Odd Ball Designs
Typesetter: Mychea
ISBN:978-1-947340-40-4
Copyright © 2019 Good2Go Publishing
Published 2019 by Good2Go Publishing
7311 W. Glass Lane • Laveen, AZ 85339
www.good2gopublishing.com
https://twitter.com/good2gobooks
G2G@good2gopublishing.com
www.facebook.com/good2gopublishing
www.instagram.com/good2gopublishing

Dedications

This book is dedicated to God, my family, and to my heart and soon-to-be wife, Jazz. I love you and will always be there for you as long as God gives me life. I promise my life on that!

J.L. Rose

This book is first dedicated to my Heavenly Father, but also to both my mother and sister. I love you both and thank you for always being there for me. Also, to J.L. Rose, you really came through with this one as you said you would, and I thank you greatly. Last and most important, to my lover and best friend: Baby, I will always and forever love you. Thank you for loving me and allowing me to love you. Thank you!

J.L. Turner

MERCENARY
IN LOVE

PROLOGUE

Sean hung up the phone after finishing a business call as he pulled up in front of his mother's house. He parked his M4 BMW and saw his mother's car, but noticed a pickup truck in the driveway.

He was unsure exactly to whom the truck belonged, but he noticed the paper tag which let him know the truck was brand new. Sean exited his BMW, started up to the front porch, and heard the television playing loudly inside the house. He used his house key that he kept after moving out, pushed open the front door, and entered the house, only to see his mother's friend, Jason, lying across the sofa.

"Diana, ya boy's here!" Jason yelled while nodding a greeting to Sean.

Sean was really not into his mother's boyfriend and paid him no attention as he headed for the kitchen and saw his mother at the stove.

"Hey, Momma!" Sean greeted, kissing Diana on the cheek before opening the refrigerator to grab a bottle of juice.

"Hi, Sean! Where you coming from?" she asked, cutting her eyes over to her son while she continued to cook.

He explained to her that he was actually just out working. He then noticed something and pushed away from the wall and approached his mother.

"Mom, what happened to you face?"

"Sean, it's—!"

"What the fuck!" Sean yelled after turning his mother's head, which allowed him to see that her left eye was swollen and changing colors.

"Sean, it's nothing, baby!" Diana tried explaining quickly, seeing the look on her son's face. "It was just a . . . Sean!"

He heard his mother scream out his name as he turned and left the kitchen, but Sean walked back out into the front room to see that Jason was no longer on the sofa.

"Sean, please!" Diana begged as she followed her son as he headed outside.

He had spotted Jason on the phone while smoking a cigarette as he stood next to the pickup truck. Sean walked out the front door and right up to Jason.

"What the fuck!" Jason began, but never finished as Sean swung and smashed a fist directly into his mouth.

He heard his mother scream and beg him to stop. But Sean beat the shit out of Jason while talking in a calm and controlled voice, even though he was past the point of being pissed off.

"This better be the last time you ever come back around here; and if I even think about your punk ass again, I may just show up and beat your ass again!"

Sean stomped and kicked Jason while still feeling some type of way, until he heard his mother yell out that she called the cops and wanted him to leave. Sean looked back to see that his mother was actually on the phone talking to the police.

Sean kicked Jason one more time before leaving his mother's front yard and walked back out to his M4. He got back into the car, but before pulling off, he looked back to see his mother down on the ground helping

Jason beside her.

Sean shook his head as he drove off, paying no attention to the neighbors that were outside watching. He just wanted to get home, get some rest, and forget about all the bullshit, when his cell phone began ringing.

Sean picked up the cell phone from the center console and answered the call upon seeing that it was his younger sister.

"Hey, Tasha! What's up, baby sis?"

Sean listened to his sister crying as she explained to him about a problem she was having with a guy that kept disrespecting her and was now putting his hands on her. Sean made the decision on the spot that he was taking a trip back to Miami to deal with the issue with his sister, but he was also hopeful he would take a little time to relax.

ONE

Thirty-four hours later

Sean was still a little tired, but he left his apartment building after driving around the previous day shopping and getting his place put together upon arriving in Miami after 2:00 p.m. He drove his new 750Li BMW, which he had traded his M4 for. He then made his way across town to meet and pick up his sister from her mother's house.

He made two stops, first to get gas and then to pick up breakfast for him and his sister. Sean then made it to his father's wife's 6-bedroom, 4.5-bath house and parked his 750Li out in front.

He climbed from the BMW and hit the locks as he walked across the front lawn and up to the front door while carrying the breakfast that he had picked up for his sister. Sean stepped onto the porch and knocked on the door as he stood trying to look through the thick snow glass.

"Sean!" Tasha screamed after throwing open the front door and then rushing into her brother's open arms.

She went up onto her toes and kissed his cheek while knocking off his hat at the same time.

"What's up, baby sis?" Sean asked, kissing his sister on the crown of her head. He then spotted Tracy standing a few feet away smiling and watching the two of them. "What's up, Tracy?"

"Hi, Sean!" Tracy replied, still smiling as both her daughter and her stepson entered the house. She accepted the kiss to the cheek that he gave her. "Boy, you look just like Jeffery with all them waves in your head. How you been, Sean?"

"I'm good, Tracy," Sean was able to say before Tasha dragged him though the house and back into her bedroom.

Once they were inside her room, Tasha went into the story that she had for him about the guy that had disrespected her and their cousin Tia.

"Who's this guy?" Sean asked as both he and Tasha began eating the breakfast he had brought. "Where's this clown live or be at?"

"He be over there on Opa-Locka a lot," she told her brother. "I know he works for Bullit Head and Bull!"

"Who?"

"That's them same dudes that Tony's been beefing

3

with over something that happened between Tony and Bull."

Sean nodded his head after listening to his sister. He then decided right then that he would get with his cousin Tony after spending a few hours with his sister.

~ ~ ~

Sean ended up at the mall at Tasha's request and spent more than $3,000 on her, buying her shit from every store into which she dragged him. He then dropped Tasha back off at her house a little after 4:00 p.m. and promised to come back through before the end of the night. He then made his way across town into Carol City and pulled up in front of his Auntie Toni's house.

Sean saw the crowd of dudes out on the front porch of his auntie's house as he was parking his 750Li.

He shut off the car and climbed out to the eyes of six guys staring hard straight at him.

"You looking for someone, boy?" Sean heard as he entered the front gate and walked up the walkway to the front porch as all six guys stood or sat up and stared at him.

"You can't hear, boy?" the dark-skinned guy with the wall of top and bottom golds spoke up, drawing Sean's attention to him.

"Who you?" Sean asked, to which he was rewarded with the chuckling from all six of the men.

Just as he was about to open his mouth again to speak, he heard a car horn blow from behind him.

He stepped back and looked behind him to see a candy-apple-red Lexus park behind his ride. He watched as his aunt and three other women got out of the car. Sean ignored the guys on the porch and walked back out front to greet her.

"Oh my God, Sean!" Toni screamed as she threw her arms up and around her nephew's neck, hugging him tightly for a few moments. She then quickly stepped back to look over his six-foot, 196-pound athletic but muscular-toned, pecan-brown-skinned body. "Damn! Yo' ass done get fine as shit, boy! What happened to you?"

"Toni, who's that, girl?" another one of the women asked as she stood up and stared Sean up and down hungrily.

"Bitch, put your eyes back up inside your head!" Toni told her girl, shooting the lonely bitch a look. "This is Big Jeff's boy! This is my nephew, Sean."

"Toni, no!" another woman cried out in disbelief.

"That's lil' Sean?"

"Ain't nothing little about his sexy ass no more!" the first woman stated, still staring at Sean with a look that he and everyone else watching could easily understand.

"Sean, come on, boy!" Toni told him, rolling her eyes at her girl before leading her nephew back into the yard and up to the front porch.

"Toni, who's that boy?" the homeboy with the golds asked while mean-mugging Sean.

"Marvin, this is Big Jeff's son, Sean," Toni told him. "You remember Sean, right?"

"Yeah!" Marvin answered, still hard staring at Sean. "I remember the youngin."

Sean paid no attention to his auntie's friend or his hard stares. He then walked through the crowd of homeboys into the house behind his Auntie Toni.

~ ~ ~

Sean kicked it with his aunt for a while, doing a little catching up since he had not seen her or the rest of the family in a while, even when he came down to visit his sister every other weekend. Sean questioned his aunt about his cousin Tony and found out that his cousin had his own place with some girl he was living with.

Sean got his cousin's address and was ready to leave, when Marvin yelled into the house that Tia had just pulled up outside.

Sean followed his auntie outside just as Tia came walking up the walkway. He stepped out from behind Toni for Tia to see him and watched as her eyes grew a bit in surprise and disbelief.

"Oh my God, Sean!" Tia screamed, taking off running, only to jump onto her cousin's arms and hug his neck tightly.

"Tia! Girl, get down off of that boy like that!" Toni told her daughter with a smile on her face.

Tia climbed down from Sean's arms and looked him over.

"Boy, when did you get here?" she asked, still smiling.

"Yesterday afternoon!" he answered. "I ain't come through yesterday because I was running all over the place trying to get my new spot on."

"You got a new place?" Tia asked him. "So you staying down here now?"

"For a while until I decide if I wanna really stay or leave again," he explained.

"You see Antonio yet?" Tia asked him. "His ass just called me a few minutes ago."

"Where he at?"

"Over there at them Overtown Apartments," Tia answered. "He, T.J., and Nina got a spot out there where they're getting their money at."

"You say Nina, huh?" Sean asked, slowly smirking upon seeing his cousin nod her head yes. "Show me where they at!"

TWO

Tia pulled up in front of her brother's trap house and saw his ass out front talking with some female while the rest of his friends stood over next to the apartment to catch customers. Tia rolled down the window on the 750Li and noticed the way Nina, T.J., and Hulk were staring at the car.

"Tony!" she called out to her brother, fully getting his attention after seeing him glance her way.

She stuck her head out of the car window so she could be seen.

"Tia, what the fuck!" Tony yelled in surprise after seeing his baby sister behind the wheel of a big-body BMW. He left the girl he was talking to and walked over to the 750Li, just as the rest of his team joined him. "Tia, whose ride you pushing?"

"What you want, Tony?" Tia asked, ignoring her brother's question. "What you call me for?"

"Girl, don't play with me!" Tony told his sister. "Who the fuck owns this car you're driving?"

"That's what I wanna know!" T.J. stated, looking over the BMW as well.

Tia sucked her teeth while trying to hide the smile that was pulling hard at her lips.

She stuck her hand out the door and pointed as she said, "This is his car, if y'all must know!"

"What?" Tony said as he and the others all spun around to see who Tia was talking about.

"Holy shit!" T.J. said in disbelief as he stood staring once he quickly recognized who was standing a few feet away leaning against the front gate of the apartment building.

"Oh my God!" Nina called out once she recognized who she was also staring at.

She took off running and jumped into her first love and hugged him tightly.

"Ain't this a bitch!" Tony stated with a smile as he started toward his cousin.

Tony waited until Nina released him, and then he embraced his cousin as well.

"What the fuck you doing back in Miami, nigga?" Tony asked.

"Tasha called, and I decided to come back home," Sean told him as he embraced T.J. and noticed the big man that was walking up with Tia. "Who's the big guy?"

"That's my nigga Hulk! He's good people, cuz!"

Tony replied as he looked back at his boy.

Sean and the big man shook hands as he dropped his arm back around Nina.

"So, who's this nigga Bull and his man Bullit Head?"

"Why you asking?" Tony questioned Sean.

Sean explained to his cousin and the rest of the team what his sister had told him about Bullit Head. Sean then looked directly at Tony.

"I hear you've already got a problem with these two. That true, cuz?"

"That's about to get handled!" Tony informed Sean, balling up his face in anger. "And Tia told me about that lil' issue. I already got something planned for both them niggas."

"You may as well call that shit off!" Sean told his

cousin. "I promised Tasha that would get handled before 9:00 p.m. tonight."

"Fam, these niggas ain't really none of them clowns you see back that way from where you from," T.J. told Sean in all seriousness.

Upon hearing T.J. and ignoring his boy, Sean looked back toward Tony.

"I'ma need a favor, Cousin. How fast can you get me a few things to deal with this issue that my sister called me out here for?"

"Cuz, is you serious?" Tony asked, seeing the look on Sean's face.

"You either gonna help me or you not. Which is it gonna be?" Sean asked, holding his cousin Tony's eyes.

~ ~ ~

Tony got his cousin everything he had requested,

but only after Sean agreed to let him and his team back him up in dealing with Bullit Head and Bull. Tony sat in the passenger seat of Hulk's Chevy Tahoe as he and the rest of the team followed behind Nina's custom-painted pink-and-chrome SRT-model Dodge Charger.

Tony recognized Bullit Head and Bull's area and instantly spotted Bull's Escalade parked in front of their trap spot. Tony caught the passenger door to Nina's Charger open and slam shut after Sean jumped out and took off at a sprint right before Nina took off up the block.

"Tony, what's up?" Hulk asked, after seeing what had just taken place.

Tony remained quiet a few moments as Hulk continued up the block. He no longer could see where Sean had gone, but he peeped Bullit Head out on the front porch as he told Hulk to follow behind Nina.

~ ~ ~

Sean smoothly and swiftly hit the fence to the house next door to the trap house that Nina had pointed out that Bull and Bullit Head ran. Sean lightly landed in the back yard of the trap house and was already sprinting by the time his Nikes touched the grass.

Sean crept up onto the back window and saw a female inside the kitchen at the stove cooking what he knew for sure was not food for the soul. He gently tried the back door and almost laughed when he found it unlocked. He then noticed the Newport buds all over the ground in front of the back door.

Once he got inside the house and quietly moved through the pantry, he peeked out around the corner into the kitchen to see the same female at the freezer. He swiftly slid up behind her and placed the Ruger .40 caliber up against the side of her head.

"Scream, or say anything until I tell you, and I'ma paint the walls with your most recent thoughts! We understand each other?"

Sean smirked once the girl nodded her head that she understood. He then asked if Bull and Bullit Head were in the house.

"Bullit Head's out front with four of his workers, and Bull's asleep on the sofa in the front room," the female squealed.

~ ~ ~

"Where the fuck is this nigga?" Tony asked as he sat beside Nina in her Charger parked on the next block behind Bull's trap spot. "What the hell he say he was going to do?"

"He only told me to wait fifteen minutes and then drive back around the front to pick him up."

"Fifteen minutes!" Tony yelled, just as the sound of someone's hammer sounded off in the near distance. He turned around in his seat and looked back at Bull's spot just as the Charger started to back up and Nina pulled off.

"What the fuck is yo' ass doing?" Tony yelled at Nina, staring at the bitch like she was crazy.

"It's fifteen minutes," was all Nina yelled back, yoking the Charger onto the next block just in time to see somebody rushing out into the street shooting back at Bull's trap spot.

"Holy shit!" Tony said after seeing blood spit out from the face of the guy in the middle of the street.

"There goes Sean!" Nina yelled as she slammed on the brakes just as he calmly walked out to the street and then over to the car carrying two duffel bags that he tossed into the back seat before climbing inside behind them.

"What the fuck just—?"

"Nina, drive!" Sean spoke up over Tony, cutting off his cousin just as he spotted Hulk's Tahoe speeding up behind them.

~ ~ ~

Sean ignored Tony the whole ride back into Overtown until he and the others were inside the apartment from which Tony and his team got their money. Sean sat down on the old sofa beside Nina as Tony, Hulk, and T.J. sat around or stood beside them. He tossed one of the two duffel bags onto the wooden coffee table.

"Normally I charge for shit like this," Sean told his people. "But since Tasha put in this request, it's on her face that I did this for free."

"What's this?" Tony asked, nodding toward the duffel bag.

Sean smirked as he looked at the bag and said, "Let's just call it payment for the tools and Bull's apology for being stupid."

Sean watched as Tony opened up the bag to see what was inside. He then pulled out his phone to see that it was almost 10:00 p.m.

"Yo, Nina," Sean called to get her attention away from the four bricks and six ounces of coke that were inside.

"Yeah, papi!" she replied with a smile upon looking

over at him. "What's up?"

He then explained to her that he needed her to take him to pick up his car because he had one other thing to handle. Sean said his goodbyes but gave his number to Tony and T.J. before he left with Nina.

Once outside, Sean followed Nina back to her car. She sat behind the wheel as he climbed into the passenger seat.

"So, what's been up with ya?" Sean asked once Nina drove off and left the trap house out of which she worked.

Nina looked over at Sean and lightly laughed as she shook her head.

"Who the hell are you?"

"What's that supposed to mean?" he asked a bit confused. "Nina, you've known me since we was babies, girl!"

"Yeah," Nina admitted. "But the Sean I know wouldn't have run up in the spot of some known killers and come back out with all their shit after murdering everybody in the damn house. So again, I ask, who are you?"

Sean chuckled after listening to her, but he decided to tell her the truth. He knew he could trust her. He broke down from when his mother first moved them to Jacksonville after his father was sent off to prison, and continued to explain how he was badly beaten by a group of boys until an older white man stepped in to help him out. Sean went on to explain how he and the white guy grew to become really close, and he found out later that the guy was actually an ex-mercenary from Russia that had relocated to the United States.

"Whoa!" Nina interrupted, laughing as she looked from the road back over at Sean. "Basically what you're telling me is that this ex-mercenary took a liking to you and in the end trained you to become a mercenary like him, Sean?"

"Let's just say that I've done my share of hired jobs for money, Nina," he told her, just as his cell phone woke up and drew his attention away from the conversation.

~ ~ ~

After picking up his car from his aunt's house, Sean kept his promise to his sister that he would see her before the night was over. He also remembered that he promised that he would stop at his grandmother's house. Sean pulled up in front of his father's wife's house and saw a few other cars parked in front of the house.

Sean climbed from the 750Li and hit the remote to lock the car doors. He then headed up to the front door just as his phone began to ring.

"I'm outside, Tasha," Sean said into the phone after answering once he saw his sister was calling.

Sean didn't even bother to knock or ring the doorbell. He stood waiting a few moments, when the front door was unlocked and snatched open by his sister and a light-skinned girl about the same age standing in front of him.

"Mamma, Sean's here!" Tasha yelled out as she pulled her brother inside.

"Who's here?" Sean asked as Tasha shut and locked the front door.

"One of Daddy's old friends," she told her brother

before she introduced the girl with her. "This is April. She's Daddy's friend's daughter."

Sean followed his sister and the young girl into the front room to see Tracy and some brown-skinned guy and woman all laughing. Sean caught his stepmother's eyes when she looked up to see him.

"Mike! Melissa!" Tracy announced as she stood up from her seat with her guest. She then grabbed Sean's hand and said, "This is my stepson, Sean."

"So this is Jeff's boy that he keeps telling me about?" the guy asked, standing up from beside his wife to hold out his hand. "It's good to finally meet you, son. The name's Michael Brown."

Sean shook the man's hand but looked over at Tracy questioningly.

Sean then looked back to the guy as he said, "Relax,

son! I'm a friend of your father's. I used to be on the

force, but I retired a little before your father went to

prison."

THREE

Sean made it back to his apartment a little after 2:00 a.m. and only had gotten in a few hours of sleep when his grandmother woke him up around 6:15 a.m. She went off about him not stopping by to see her since he had stopped to see Toni and his stepmother, Tracy.

Sean got up and got dressed in black metallic jeans, a white Hanes T-shirt, and some all-white Air Force Ones. He then snatched up his black-on-white Yankees fitted cap and black blazer-style leather jacket before heading out the door.

He rode the elevator down to the parking garage and stepped off once he arrived on the lower level. He almost ran into a female that came rushing off the elevator next to the one off of which he had stepped.

"Excuse me!" she yelled back to him as she continued jogging through the parking garage.

Sean paid the woman little attention and continued to his car, just as his phone woke up and rang from his Bluetooth.

"Yeah! Who this?"

"Where you at, papi?"

Sean recognized Nina's voice and explained that he was leaving his place and heading over to his grandmother's house to see her for a little while.

"Tony wants you to come by the spot when you get a chance, but I also want you to meet somebody. Can you ride with me somewhere tomorrow morning?"

"What time?"

"Early, papi!"

"Just remind me later tonight."

After finishing up his phone call with Nina, his phone began to ring again. He recognized the name from the night before, but not the number.

"What's up, Detective?"

"Sean!" Michael replied with a light laugh from the way he had answered the phone. "Boy, you are your father's son. You got a minute?"

"Can we meet in ten minutes? I wanna talk with you about a few things."

"Can it wait until later? I'm about to meet with my grandmother for a while."

"How about twelve noon?"

"I'll call you back at 3:00 p.m.," Sean told the retired detective. "Is this the number you're gonna be at?"

"You can call me at the number I gave you last night, son."

After hanging up the phone with Michael Brown and wondering what the man wanted to talk to him about, Sean pushed the thought to the back of his mind and turned down the street toward his grandmother's house.

~ ~ ~

Sean visited his grandmother, Ma'Pearl, and actually enjoyed his time with the woman that gave birth to his father. While enjoying lunch, they first conversed about his mother and then his father, and then onto the topic of what woman he was seriously seeing.

"Ma'Pearl, I'm really not seeing anybody right

now," he told her.

She then interrupted and said, "Baby, I've got someone I want you to meet."

"Ma'Pearl, I'm not really—!"

"Boy, I'm not asking you nothing," she told her grandson in a tone used with all of her kids and grandkids when she was not going to take no for an answer. "I expect you to be here at this house tonight at 10:15 p.m. Are we clear, young man?"

Sean sighed as he sat back in his seat and gave in.

"Yes ma'am. I'll be here, Ma'Pearl."

~ ~ ~

Sean left his grandmother's house a little after 1:00 p.m. to meet up with his cousin, Tony, to see what he wanted to talk to him about. Sean pulled up in his BMW in front of Tony's trap spot and saw Hulk posted out front.

"What's up, Tony's cousin?" Hulk greeted Sean after he climbed from his car and started walking up to the apartment.

"It's just Sean, playboy!" Sean told the big man, shaking up with him. "Tony inside?"

"Yeah!" Hulk answered, nodding his head back toward the apartment door.

After leaving Hulk in front of the apartment, Sean entered after knocking once. He saw his cousin and Nina inside bagging up what looked like ounces of coke.

"What's up, cuz?" Tony said with a smile as he set down the half-bagged ounce he was working on.

Tony stood up to embrace his cousin. After releasing him, Sean then looked over at Nina, who was still packing up the ounce she was working on.

"What's up, Nina?" he asked.

Nina looked up from her work to see Sean's smoky-gray eyes staring down at her. She broke into a smile after realizing what he was waiting on. She stopped what she was doing to stand up and give him a hug.

"Hi, papi!"

"You two a trip!" Tony stated, shaking his head and smiling at the two of them. "I still don't understand why you two still ain't get together yet. It's easy to see that Nina's fucked up about you, cuz, and you're feeling her."

"Nina's gonna always be my girl," Sean said, which caused her to blush and cut her eyes from him back to the work. He smiled and winked his eye at her before focusing his attention back to his cousin. "So, what's up, Tony? What you wanna talk to me about?"

After finishing up the ounce that he was putting together, Tony turned his attention toward Sean.

"So, tell me something, cuz. This shit you pulled off yesterday was on the news. They said there was six dead inside the house and one dead outside the front of the house, which gives a total of seven people that were inside. Now tell me how the hell you was able to walk up inside that house by yo' damn self and kill seven muthafuckers, when only one of them was a woman and even she was strapped."

"I caught 'em slipping, I guess," Sean told Tony with a smirk.

"Bullshit, Sean!" Tony told him, sitting back in his seat while still staring at his cousin. "What the fuck was you on back in Riverside, cuz?"

"What you asking, cuz?" Sean questioned, holding his cousin's stare.

Tony remained silent for a few moments and held Sean's eyes.

"You done went and became a jack boy or something?" Tony finally spoke up.

Sean chuckled at Tony's question and then answered, "Relax, Cousin. I don't do the robbing thing. Not enough paper for me to make a living with my lifestyle."

Tony nodded his head and believed his cousin, but he knew there was something more to Sean than his cousin was letting on.

Tony made a decision right then and said, "So, what's up, cuz? You coming on with the team, or what?"

"Tony, you already know I'm not into that!"

"Chill, Sean!" Tony said, holding up his hands to get Sean to hold on. "I'm not talking about selling nothing. I'm talking about with security. After the way I saw you handle that burner yesterday and hit that fool out on the street while you was still up on the porch, I knew you'd had some type of training with guns. So what's up? You down with the team, right?"

"Tony, look!" Sean started, sighing as he sat forward in his seat. "You know I love you and whenever or wherever you need me, I always got you. But I work alone, Cousin. No disrespect to you or the team, but I do things a lot different than you guys may. I tell you what, though, whenever you guys do have a problem and want it handled quickly, then give me a call. Understand, though, that last night was free because of Tasha and what you did for me, but from now on, family or not, I'ma need my paper for whatever job you guys ask me to take care of for y'all. We understand each other?"

"I understand ya, Cuz," Tony replied as he and Sean stood up from their seats to embrace each other. "Where you about to slide to now?"

"I gotta meet up with one of my pop's old friends," Sean informed him while checking the time on the Movado watch on his wrist.

~ ~ ~

Sean contacted Michael Brown and agreed on a location for the two of them to meet. Sean arrived at a small diner and recognized the Cadillac DTS that was parked in the lot from last night at Tracy's house. He parked his BMW and then climbed out to see Michael waving from one of the booth windows.

He entered the diner a few moments later and waved off the blonde-haired waitress that started walking toward him when he entered. Sean made his way over to Michael's booth and slid in across from the detective.

"Thanks for coming, Sean," Michael began the conversation. "I asked you here because I wanted to talk to you about a possible future in business together. Are you interested in hearing more?"

"I'm listening," Sean told Michael while relaxing back in his seat and focusing on the retired detective.

Michael began explaining his relationship with Sean's father, which was watching out and covering for his father, all while he was not only having cocaine brought into the states but also sold throughout all of Miami and ten other cities across Florida. Michael finished up by asking Sean his choice of product and if he was interested in doing business as well.

"Well!" Sean began, sitting forward and resting his arms on top of the table. "First, thanks for considering me as a business partner due to the history between you and my father, but I'm going to have to turn down the offer. I'm not into that type of business my father was into."

"You're not?" Michael asked with a surprised look on his face.

"No, I'm not!" Sean repeated. "Let's just say that I'm the person you'll call when you're having a problem you want taken care of quietly and quickly. Get my drift, Detective?"

Michael understood clearly what the young man was telling him, and he now sat looking at Sean in a different light.

"So, if what you're saying is true, Sean, what is your price?"

"Depends on the job!" Sean replied. "Are you looking for help with a problem, Detective?"

"I may have a few offers for you," Michael admitted. "I tell you what, though, give me a few days and I'll contact you again."

Sean nodded his head and stood from his seat. With nothing else to say, he left Michael Brown inside the diner.

~ ~ ~

Sean showed up at his grandmother's house five minutes earlier than she had ordered him to. He arrived with food for the two of them. He parked his 750Li and was climbing from the car just as he noticed the headlights from a Chevy Malibu slowly making its way up the block in his direction.

He slid his hand down to his side while holding the bag of food in his left hand, contemplating whether or not to pull out his Glock 17 that was inside the back holster under the jacket he was wearing. He watched the driver's side window slide down as the Malibu slowed to a stop in front of him.

"Ummm, is this Ms. Pearl Carter's house?" the female inside the car asked him.

Sean was unsure exactly why the female looked familiar, but he asked, "Who you?"

"I'm Mia. My grandmother is friends with Ms. Pearl, and I'm supposed to come over and pick up something from her for my grandmother."

"Mia, that you, baby?" Mia and Sean heard a voice from the porch. They both looked toward the front door of the house and saw Ma'Pearl standing outside. "Come on inside, Mia, and bring my hard-headed grandson with you."

~ ~ ~

"How you doing, Mia?" Ma'Pearl greeted and hugged the young woman.

"I'm fine, Ms. Pearl," Mia answered as she released the older woman.

"Well, give me a few minutes, Mia!" Ma'Pearl told her. "These pies are just about finished. My grandson can keep you company while I'm finishing up in the kitchen."

Sean watched his grandmother and saw the look

she shot him. He then shook his head and figured out what she was up to.

"I apologize for not introducing myself outside," Sean said, getting Mia's attention as she sat looking around the front room. "I'm Sean."

"Mia!" she replied, shaking his hand and trying not to stare into his eyes too long.

"You've got an accent. Up North?" he asked. "New Jersey, right?"

"Great ears!" Mia told him with a smile and surprise. "Did you really get that from the way I talk, or was it a guess?"

"People from New York and New Jersey speak almost alike but say a few words totally differently. By your accent, I knew you was from New Jersey."

"Impressive!" she told him while still smiling. "So

where are you from, Sean?"

"What makes you think I'm not from right here in Miami?"

"Well, you don't speak like people from Miami, but also because I knew you would be here, Sean," Mia admitted, "My grandmother does not know how to keep a secret. She and your grandmother suggested hooking us up so we could meet."

"And you agreed to it?"

"I really don't know why, but I guess I did since I'm sitting here talking to you. Besides, I'm new in this city and don't really know too many people here; and considering that you're kind of cute, I would consider letting you take me out."

"Kind of cute, huh?" Sean repeated, smiling across at Mia. He shook his head and said, "So, since you're considering letting me take you out, I guess it's safe to ask you for your number then, huh?"

"I was wondering what took you so long!" Mia joked, only to receive a laugh from Sean as he pulled out his own cell phone.

~ ~ ~

Ma'Pearl quickly got on her phone and called her friend Mary. She heard the entire conversation that was going on in her front room a few feet away. She had a smile on her face the whole time.

"Hello!"

"Mary, it's Pearl. Girl, we did it!"

"We did? Oh good! You mean they actually hooked up, Pearl?"

"They're in my front room as we speak laughing and talking."

"So they actually like each other?"

"Mary, ain't you listening to me, old woman? They're in my front room laughing and talking right now. Mia even gave my grandson her number so they can go out soon."

"Is that Ms. Washington?" a voice called out behind her.

Ma'Pearl jumped in surprise after hearing the question and quickly recognized the voice of her grandson. She slowly turned around and was shocked to see not only her grandson but also Mia standing right behind her inside the doorway to the kitchen.

"Mary, I think we're busted, girl!"

Sean shook his head and laughed along with Mia and Ma'Pearl. Sean then leaned toward his grandmother and kissed her on the cheek.

FOUR

"**J**effery Carter!"

Upon hearing his name called out over the intercom speaker inside the dormitory while watching college football that early Saturday afternoon, Big Jeff spun around in his seat on the bench inside the dayroom to look back up at the officer station. He saw the dorm officer holding up a written sign that read Visitation.

He was surprised he was receiving a visit this weekend when he knew his wife was already due to visit the following weekend. But Big Jeff got up and headed back to his cell to get himself together for his visit.

After taking a quick shower and putting on his

visitation blue uniform and wax-shined boots, Big Jeff ran the brush across his short, wavy salt-and-pepper hair before leaving his cell and picking up his visitation pass that allowed him to get up front.

About ten minutes after arriving at the visitation park and being strip-searched, Big Jeff got himself back together before walking out onto the visitation floor.

"Daddy!"

Big Jeff smiled when he recognized the voice as soon as he walked out onto the floor. He spotted his baby girl rushing toward him with a big smile on her beautiful face and her arms open wide.

"Hey, baby girl!" Big Jeff said, catching his daughter in a bear hug and holding her tightly for a few moments before letting her go long enough to look her over. "You're looking good, baby girl. Where's ya momma at?"

"She's waiting with Sean."

"With who?" Big Jeff asked, looking at his daughter with an unsure look. "What did you just say, Tasha?"

"Daddy, look!" Tasha told him with a big grin as she pointed toward where both her mother and brother were sitting.

Big Jeff spotted his wife as soon as he looked to where his daughter was pointing. He froze when his eyes landed on the young man seated beside his wife and staring directly back at him.

"I'll be damned!" Big Jeff said aloud as he and Tasha made their way across the room, where he first greeted his wife who stood up to give him a hug and kiss.

"Hey, baby!" Tracy said, smiling up at her husband.

After speaking to his wife for a brief moment, Big Jeff turned his attention to his oldest child, who sat calmly in his seat waiting until he was spoken to.

"Long time, no see, Son."

Sean lifted his head and met his father's smoke-gray eyes, just like his own. Sean pushed back his seat and then stood up to greet his father. He threw his arms around him in a hug.

"What's up, Pops?"

Once everyone was seated at the table that was selected, Big Jeff addressed his son first.

"So, what's been going on, Son? When you get to Miami?"

"I'm living in Miami now, Pops," he informed his father before running down the short version of why he had relocated to the city.

Big Jeff shook his head at his son and showed a small smile before he asked, "So what you been up to since I saw you last with your mother? How's everything been going? You look like you're doing good out there for yourself, boy."

"Let's just say that I've been doing pretty good for myself, Pops," Sean stated with a smirk.

"Honey, you want something to eat?" Tracy asked her husband while standing up from her seat to go to the food window.

"Just grab me anything," Big Jeff replied as he began to pull off his ID for her to pay for their food.

"Keep your ID, baby," Tracy told him with a grin. "Sean gave me money for all of us to eat."

Big Jeff looked at his wife and daughter as they

walked away, before he focused back on his son.

"What's really going on with you, Sean? I haven't seen you since you were fifteen, and your mother brought you up here to see me last, and now you're back and giving my wife money to feed me and my family. Talk, boy!"

"Let's go outside, Pops!" Sean suggested, standing from his seat as his father followed his lead.

~ ~ ~

Once outside, both Tracy and Tasha sat under the hut at a concert table used by the visitors and the inmates that were receiving visits. Sean walked around the hut with his father and admitted everything to him about what he was into and how he had gotten into taking contract jobs for a living.

Big Jeff laughed lightly after listening to his twenty-five-year-old son.

"So, my son is a trained hitman. Is that what you're telling me?"

"Something like that!" Sean answered before he changed the subject. "Pops, you know somebody named Michael Brown?"

"What about 'im?" Big Jeff asked while glancing over at his son.

Sean explained to his father about the meeting and the offer the retired detective had made to him.

"Can he really be trusted?"

"You thinking about taking him up on an offer if he makes one?" Big Jeff asked.

"New city and new clients, Pops," Sean stated. "I gotta build clientele some type of way, and why not start with the help of someone like Michael?"

After hearing his son and agreeing with him on a business level, Big Jeff then replied, "I tell you what, Sean. Handle your business, but trust no damn body, Son. Make sure you know everything that's going on and everybody that's a part of everything you're getting into. You get what I'm saying, boy?"

"I got you, Pops!"

"Good! Now let's get something to eat. I'm hungry as hell!"

~ ~ ~

Sean made it back to the city after leaving the prison and dropped Tracy and his sister off at home. He then headed to his own place in order to rest since he was up very early to drive out to see his father. He was at least twenty minutes from his apartment building when his cell phone began ringing through his

Bluetooth.

"Yeah!"

"Sean, what the hell happened to you? I thought you were going to go with me this morning to pick up my sister?"

Sean recognized Nina's voice, but he was unable to remember ever agreeing to go with her to pick up her sister. He didn't admit that he didn't remember; instead, he told Nina that he was summoned by his father to show up at the prison to see him.

Nina sucked her teeth, but she was unable to fight with Sean after Big Jeff called for him, so she asked, "Sean, where you at now?"

"On my way home."

"Well, gimme your address. We're on our way over there now."

Sean really just wanted to sleep and was in no mood for visitors, but he refused to tell Nina that. Instead, he gave her the address and room number to his apartment.

Sean arrived at his apartment building a short while later and slowed the BMW truck that he rented for the trip to visit his father. While he pulled into the parking garage, he recognized the car that was turning in front of him.

"Mia?" Sean stated aloud, unsure if it was really her Malibu he was looking at as he trailed the car into the parking garage.

When he saw the Malibu park a few spaces down from where he was parking, he sat inside the truck and waited a few moments until he did, in fact, see Mia carrying Walmart bags in both arms walking past the truck.

He shut off the truck, got out, walked around the back end, and called out to her to slow up. She looked back over her shoulder and smiled after a brief moment once she recognized him.

~ ~ ~

"Sean, what are you doing here?" Mia asked in surprise.

She was happy to see him, but she also wondered how he knew where she lived.

"Actually, I live here too," he told her as he relieved her of the two bags she was carrying. "I have a place on the tenth floor."

"You mean you have a condo on the tenth floor?" Mia corrected him, cutting her eyes up at him with a smile. "Ain't nothing but condos up that high."

"I guess!" he replied with a smirk showing as they stopped in front of the elevator.

"Excuse me," Mia apologized after bumping into Sean and dropping her keys. She squatted, picked them up, and stood up to face him. "Wait a second! This is crazy, Sean. I actually remember you now!"

"Remember me how?" he asked, a little confused.

"Yesterday morning, I was rushing to take care of something," she explained. "I got down here and was rushing off the elevator and—!"

"And almost ran me over!" Sean finished her sentence. "I did think you looked familiar at first. I thought it was because you looked just like Nia Long from *Friday* with Ice Cube and Chris Tucker. You know, with the whole short cut hairstyle. But, yeah, I remember you now."

"This is crazy!" Mia said as the two of them stepped onto the elevator.

"Naw!" Sean said as the door was closing and drawing Mia's attention onto him again.

"Excuse me?"

"I said naw!" he repeated as he held Mia's hazel brown eyes. "It's not crazy we met yesterday."

"Then what was it, Sean, since you seem to know?" she asked him with a smile.

"I'll let you know soon!" Sean told her in all seriousness as he continued holding her eyes. "Just remember you asked me that question when it's time for me to answer."

Mia suddenly felt hot as she stood locking eyes with Sean. She tore her eyes free and looked at the changing elevator numbers as she suddenly became aware that she was fanning herself because of how hot she felt being so close to Sean.

Once the doors opened on her floor, she noticed that Sean was also getting off the elevator with her bags. Mia then started to thank him and take her bags, only to instead begin walking up the hallway and stopping in front of her apartment. After unlocking and opening the front door, she never got the chance to say or do anything else as Sean stepped around her and walked inside.

"Come on in, why don't ya?"

"Nice setup you got here," Sean told her as she closed and locked the door behind her.

"Thanks!" Mia replied as she took the bags from Sean and then headed into the kitchen.

Mia set the bags onto the counter and looked up at

the sound of the television being turned on. She stood staring in shock upon seeing Sean in her den sitting on her sofa and changing the channels on her TV looking for something to watch.

She shook her head, unable to keep from laughing at what she was seeing. She then turned her focus back to putting away her groceries.

~ ~ ~

About five minutes later, Mia walked into her open den where Sean was watching television. He looked up as Mia handed him a bottle of juice.

"Are you staying for dinner?" she asked, dropping down beside him on the sofa.

"Can we do it tomorrow?" he asked her before he explained, "I've got friends coming over, so I can't stay long. I do want to take you up on that offer though."

Mia stared hard at Sean and shook her head.

"You are something else, Sean! What time are you going to be here for dinner, boy?" she asked with a smile and shake of the head.

After coming to an agreement on the time that the two of them would have dinner together, both Sean and Mia sat talking and laughing while paying no attention to the time until they were interrupted by his phone ringing.

Mia was disappointed when Sean told her he needed to go and his friends were up at his condo. She didn't expect it when he asked her if she wanted to come up and meet his friends with him.

Accepting his offer only because Sean would not take no for an answer, Mia asked for a few minutes as she rushed to her bedroom to change into different clothes.

~ ~ ~

Nina wondered where the hell Sean's ass was after just hanging up the phone with him eight minutes earlier. She pulled out her phone again to call him, just as she heard the elevator doors open on the floor.

She saw a middle-aged couple get off the elevator instead of it being Sean. She began to pull up his number again, when she heard her sister asking where Sean was.

"I'm about to call his ass again now!" Nina replied as she began to call his phone again.

She then looked up at the sound of the elevator doors again, but this time she saw a Nia Long lookalike step off the elevator. Nina started to look back at her phone when she caught a glimpse of Sean getting off the elevator behind the girl.

"Oh shit! Damn, that nigga's ass is fine, Nina!"

Nina heard her sister, but she was too busy staring at Sean and the fake-ass Nia Long as they walked together laughing. In fact, the two were unaware that Nina and her sister were even standing in front of his apartment door. Nina heard herself angrily call Sean's name, which got both his and the bitch's attention.

"Nina, what's up?" Sean asked, smiling as he leaned in and gave her a kiss on top of her head. He then introduced Mia. "Nina, this is Mia. Mia, this is an old friend from back when I was young. This is Nina."

"Hi!" Mia said, holding out her hand to Nina.

Nina paid no attention to Mia's hand and looked angrily at Sean. In Spanish, she asked him who the fuck Mia was and why she was even up at his apartment.

"Nina, what's up with the attitude? Mia's good people, and she's with me!" Sean calmly responded back in Spanish.

"Oh, she's with you, huh?" Nina asked in Spanish, but continued in English, "Since the bitch is with you, I'm outta here!"

Sean watched Nina storm off with the Spanish female that he assumed was her sister. He then shook his head in confusion but looked at Mia and saw the look on her face.

"Why didn't you tell me you had a girlfriend, Sean?" Mia asked him, upset.

"Whoa!" Sean said as he grabbed her hands and turned and opened his apartment door. He pulled her inside and then locked the door behind them. "First of all, I didn't tell you Nina was a girlfriend because she isn't nor has she ever been. We've only been friends and nothing more. I have nothing to hide from you; and if you feel as if you can't trust or believe that I'm really interested in you, then we can end things now before we grow any closer than we already have. What you gonna do?"

Mia stared into Sean's eyes with her face balled up and her arms folded across her chest. She shoved a finger into his chest and said, "Sean, I'm telling you now. If you lie to me one time or if I find out you're playing with me, I am going to seriously hurt you. Don't make me fall for you, and this is nothing but—!"

Sean cut Mia off after stepping into her and kissing her on the lips. He slid his arms around her slim and toned waist and pulled her body up against his as he felt her arms slide up and around his neck while the kiss deepened between them.

Sean broke the kiss after a few minutes after hearing Mia's moans in protest right before she opened her eyes.

"Still questioning whether I'm playing or not?" he asked with a sly smile.

FIVE

Sean kicked it with Mia for the next three days, getting to know each other and spending as much time together as they could, until Michael Brown returned. Sean received another call from the retired detective just after receiving a call from Mia letting him know that she was going in for an interview at a new job for which she was applying.

After agreeing to meet up with Michael by 11:15 a.m. at the same diner, Sean got dressed in a casual Polo outfit and then stepped into some Polo loafers. He picked up his black leather jacket as he texted Mia to let her know to call him later after she finished her interview.

Sean locked up his place and took the elevator

down to the parking garage. As he headed for his car, his cell phone began to ring from inside his pocket. He dug out his Bluetooth and pushed it into his ear to speak into.

He then answered his call: "Yeah!"

"Sean?"

"Mom!" he responded, after recognizing her voice. "You okay?"

"I'm fine, Sean. Where are you?"

"I'm in Miami with Tasha and Tracy."

Diana was quiet for a few moments after hearing where her son was staying.

She sighed loudly into the phone and then said, "Have you spoken to your father yet?"

"I saw him last Saturday," Sean confessed. "He asked about you and told me to tell you what's up."

They continued their call that lasted the entire drive over to the diner where he was meeting Michael. Sean then sat in the parking lot in his car speaking with his mother on the phone while watching the retired detective watching him from inside the diner from the same booth as last time.

After finishing his call with his mother, after giving her his word to at least call her twice a week to let her hear his voice, Sean hung up the phone and then finally climbed from his 750Li, hit the remote locks, and started toward the diner.

He again waved off a different waitress after entering the diner. He then walked up to Michael's table and sat down across from him, just as he did the last time.

"Is everything okay?" Michael asked. "You sat in

the car a while before coming inside."

"I was on the phone with my mother," Sean admitted.

"Diana?" Michael stated with a smile. "How is she?"

"Good!" Sean replied, but then changed the conversation from his mother to why they were even meeting. "So, what's the meaning of this meeting, Detective?"

Michael nodded his head and leaned back into his seat. He laid his hands on top of the table as he began.

"The last time we met, you stated that your services were for hire. Are they still up for offer?"

"Who's the target, Detective?"

Michael picked up the brown folder that sat beside him on the bench. He laid the folder on top of the table and then slid it across the table in front of Sean.

"His name's William Cox."

Sean read through the folder that was given to him which provided information on a thirty-three-year-old judge. Sean shifted his eyes over the paperwork and saw the name of the person that was hiring him.

"So, who's this Larry Summit?"

"It's all in the folder," Michael told Sean before he added, "A few years ago, Larry was sentenced to fifty-six years in prison for a capital murder by the same judge you saw mentioned in the folder. The thing is, when Larry was sentenced, he was still a married man to a model named Rachell Woodman, but as soon as our friend Larry went to jail—!"

"Cox is fucking the model?" Sean finished for Michael.

Michael nodded his head that Sean was correct, before he added, "Our friend Larry is willing to pay $45,000 for this job."

"Does this guy have the money?" Sean wanted to know.

"Let's just say that even though our friend is locked away, he's still $65 million strong," Michael explained with a smile.

Sean nodded his head after hearing that bit of information. He then sat silently a few moments just thinking.

"Tell your client that if he wants the job done, I'm going to charge him $500,000. Get with me after you've got an answer."

Sean then stood up from the booth and walked away from the table, leaving Michael still seated. Sean caught a glimpse of Michael on his phone in mid-conversation with whom he assumed was the client, Larry Summit.

~ ~ ~

Sean was only three minutes away from the diner when his cell phone woke up. He answered the phone and was not surprised when Michael's voice came over the line.

"Our friend is willing to pay half of what you're asking!" Michael explained to Sean.

"What part of what I said didn't you catch the first time I said it, Detective?" Sean asked Michael. "Your client wants what he wants, and I want what he was just told I want. It's not up for negotiation!"

"I hear what you're saying."

"I'll pay it!" another voice spoke up, cutting off

Michael. "I'm not sure exactly who you are, due to our friend's unwillingness to give me your name, but how do I know you can handle the job correctly?"

"I'll tell you what! I'm going to give you the information where to send the money. You don't have to send anything until the job is done. But understand that when the job is finished, if the money isn't there, I will come to pay you a visit, and I'm not speaking of a normal visitation either. Do we understand each other?"

"You handle the job and the money will be there, my friend," Larry told him, but then said, "One more question though."

"I'm listening," Sean replied.

"How will I know when the job is completed?"

"Just watch the news. It'll be the headline and top

story on every news channel."

After hanging up with both Michael and his first new client, Sean got right back onto the phone and intended first to find a hotel in Orlando and then set things up to have a package shipped out to the hotel by UPS for himself once he got to town.

~ ~ ~

Sean spent most of the afternoon with his sister, once she got out of school. He had surprised her by picking her up and taking her out to eat. He finally received a text message from Mia a little after 8:00 p.m. apologizing for not calling him. Her text explained that she went in for an interview, only to end up starting work the same day. He sent her a text message back explaining that he needed to go out of town on some business, but he would be back in a day.

After leaving his sister's house at 11:35 p.m. and heading back to his place only to change clothes, Sean spent less than ten minutes inside his condo. He put on all black, grabbed his black leather jacket, and headed back out the front door.

He climbed into his 750Li and drove over to Enterprise, where his rental car was already waiting for him. He parked his BMW, picked up the rental car, and drove out of the lot three minutes later in a black Lexus E350.

~ ~ ~

Sean made it to Orlando by 3:35 a.m. the next morning, only stopping once for gas. He pulled up into the Best Western Hotel where he had mailed his package. He didn't even bother parking in a space. Instead, he left his car running outside the front door.

Once he was inside the hotel, he walked up to the desk, just as a middle-aged man was walking off. Sean calmly and respectfully introduced himself under the name that the hotel room and package were listed and asked for his package.

"Do you have any ID, sir?" the red-headed male clerk asked.

Sean showed the fake ID with Alex Hill's name on it and received his package. He then turned and walked back out of the hotel.

Once he was inside the Lexus, he tossed the UPS package onto the passenger seat and pulled off. He then picked up the brown folder he was given with all the information on Judge William Cox.

~ ~ ~

Sean reached Sanford no more than fifteen

minutes after leaving the Best Western in Orlando. He drove out to Riverfront where he knew the judge lived in a high-rise condo with Larry Summit's wife.

He noted that the building was protected by security and a security gate, so Sean drove around the building to get a good look at the area. He noticed that even the back parking garage entrance had a security booth posted with an armed guard.

Sean came up with an idea and pulled off from in front of the apartment parking garage entrance, only to park up the street behind a pickup truck that was parked in front of a dark-colored house that had a junkyard with shit everywhere. Sean picked up the UPS package, opened it, and pulled out the .25 automatic and silencer inside.

He checked the magazine to make sure he had the

thing fully loaded, and then attached the silencer to it before sliding the piece into the back holster he always wore. Sean then climbed from the Lexus and closed the door behind him, but he left the door unlocked.

Sean headed back around to the parking garage entrance and caught the security guard just as the guy was stepping out of the booth.

"You can't come in through here!" the guard told Sean as he stood blocking the entrance.

"Listen, I just!" Sean began before he lowered his voice to just a whisper, which caused the guard to lean forward to try to hear what he was saying.

"What was that?"

Sean moved before the security guard could see or realize what was happening. He smashed an open-handed punch straight to the guard's face, which dazed him. He then caught the guard before he could hit the ground; and with a swift twist, Sean broke the guard's neck.

He dragged the dead security guard back over and into the booth, where Sean laid him on the floor inside. He then backed out and closed the door behind him.

After leaving the booth and walking over to the elevator, Sean hit the call button and then looked at his watch and saw that it was 5:10 a.m.

Once the elevator door opened, Sean took it to the ninth floor and got off as soon as the doors opened. He found Room #907 and knocked loud enough for whoever was inside to hear him.

Sean heard movement behind the door and stared through the peephole, just as a voice asked, "Who is it?"

Sean swung the .25 up and aimed at the peephole.

Phiss!

After hearing the sound of a body hit the ground at dead weight, Sean shot the lock on the door, just as he heard the screaming from a woman inside.

Sean pushed open the front door with his left hand as he entered the condo, leading with his right hand that held the .25 automatic. He spotted the woman inside the kitchen on the wall phone.

Phiss! Phiss!

He shot the phone, which caused the woman to jump and scream when she saw him.

Sean simply said, "Larry sends his love."

~ ~ ~

Larry received the call five minutes ago that he had been waiting for. He sat inside the dayroom of his dormitory at the federal prison. He then waved off a few of his associates that were trying to talk to him.

He focused on the television and watched until the early morning news began. Larry then looked at the clock inside the officer station and saw that it was almost 6:00 a.m.

"About damn time!" he stated, upon seeing that the news was beginning.

Larry sat forward in his seat just as the first three stories were given, before a preview started with the top story.

Larry broke out in a smile after the first few minutes of the news story upon hearing that Judge William Cox and Rachell Woodman were killed around 5:53 a.m. Larry sat and listened to the details of their deaths and how an anonymous call was made that reported the murder of the judge and model.

After hearing enough of the story, Larry stood up from his seat and smiled. He then returned to his room and asked his roommate to step out, explaining that he needed the room for a few minutes.

After his roommate was gone and he covered up the window, Larry got on his cell phone that he kept hidden and called up Michael Brown with a smile on his face.

"Michael Brown here."

"Brown, this is Larry."

"I'm assuming you saw the news? I'm watching it as we speak."

"I've seen enough!" Larry stated, still smiling and feeling joyful. "Let your guy know that I'll be sending his payment, but add that I'll be putting a little extra in with it."

SIX

Sean checked on his money after receiving a call from Michael, who let him know what Larry Summit had to say about the hit. He also noticed that Larry had added another $100,000 to the initial $500,000 payment.

Sean then returned to his normal routine. He first checked up on his sister in the afternoon, and then tried calling Mia later on in the day but only got her voice mail.

He rode around Overtown to see what was up with his cousin Tony and the rest of his friends. Sean was not surprised when he saw all of them outside in front of the apartment.

"God damn, nigga!" Tony yelled out to Sean as his

cousin was climbing out of the BMW. "We been trying to get at you all day. Where the fuck you been?"

"I bet his ass has been with that bitch!" Nina said loud enough that Sean heard her.

He heard her but ignored her, since he knew the type of time she was on. He embraced his cousin and then shook up with Hulk and T.J.

"What's been up though? What y'all been looking for me for?"

"First, we heard about this fool Bull's brother supposedly out looking to find out who's behind his murder and talking about that he has $20,000 for whoever knows who did it. But he has another $30,000 for whoever finds and kills the person who killed Bull."

"Who's this guy?" Sean asked with his faced all balled up.

"Dude's name is Marcus," T.J. answered. "He got out of prison for attempted murder and drug trafficking. Word is, he still got a little paper."

"Fuck that nigga though, cuz!" Tony stated with a wave of his hand. "That nigga ain't gonna find out shit, so fuck 'im. I wanna know what's up. You rolling with us tonight?"

"Where at?" Sean asked, peeping the Acura that was coming down the block. He looked back and watched the car as it slowed in front of the apartment, and he saw the same female step out who was with Nina at his condo that night.

"Tony, what's up?" Maria called out, waving him out to the car.

"Hold up real quick, cuz!" Tony informed Sean while jogging out to the Acura.

"Nina!" Sean called out, only to be ignored.

He called out to her again, and this time he received a really nasty look.

"What the fuck you want, Sean?" Nina asked angrily, with arms folded across her chest as she mean-mugged him.

"Come here!" Sean told her as he stepped away from the rest of the group. "Let me holla at you real quick."

Nina sucked her teeth as she walked over to stand in front of him.

She looked up at him and with attitude said, "What do you want, Sean?"

"So you still gonna keep up with this attitude, huh?"

"What do you care?"

J.L. ROSE & J.L. TURNER

"So it's like that now?"

"Nigga, you made it like this when you had that bitch at your apartment and you knew I was coming."

"Whoa!" Sean said in surprise. "So you was really pissed because I brought Mia home with me?"

"Sean, you wanna stand here and really play with me, nigga?" Nina asked as she stepped closer to Sean. "Yo' ass knows damn well what's wrong with me; and if you keep playing me for stupid, we gonna have a real problem out here today."

"Wow!" Sean chuckled lightly as he held up his hands to keep Nina back. "All right, Nina! You mad because I brought Mia, but what I honestly don't know is why though."

Upon seeing that Sean was dead-ass serious, Nina sucked her teeth and started to walk away before she

90

stopped and turned back toward him.

"You know what, Sean? I don't even know why I'm mad at you. It's not like I've ever told you what was really up, but I tell you what though. You may wanna keep a close eye on that new bitch you messing with. She ain't right!"

Sean was caught off guard by what Nina had just told him. He started to call out to her, only to see her climb into the Acura with her sister.

Sean walked back over to where Tony, Hulk, and T.J. stood. He walked up, only for Tony to go right back into the conversation they were having before the Acura pulled up.

"So what's up, Cuz? You rolling with us tonight or what?"

"Where we going?" Sean asked, taking out his cell

phone, pulling up Mia's number, and sending her a text.

"There's something going on at Club Palace," Tony told Sean. "What I've been hearing is that this nigga Luther Simmons is supposed to be having a birthday party there and is having everyone there."

"Who the fuck is Luther Simmons?" Sean asked, looking back at his phone to see that Mia was responding.

He read her message letting him know that she couldn't see him that night, and explained that she had something to handle with her job. She would try to call him the next day. Sean felt a strong build-up of anger when he remembered what Nina had just told him about Mia.

"So what's up, Cuz?" Tony asked again. "We going

or what?"

"Yeah!" Sean answered as he turned to walk away. He then called back over his shoulder, "Hit me on my phone and let me know what time we leaving. I gotta handle something real quick."

~ ~ ~

"Mia, are you listening?"

Mia lost her train of thought and looked from her phone book over to her partner as they were supposed to be going over their reports. She focused back on what was being discussed and picked up the papers in front of her.

"Ummm, yes. I've agreed to join Mr. Simmons tonight at his birthday party, but I'm still unsure whether his business associates will show up or not."

"Did you not say that it was his birthday, Agent

Washington?" the male voice on the speakerphone asked as both Mia and her partner, Jennifer Thomas, sat on each side of the telephone speaking with their boss.

"Yes, sir!" Mia replied, but then stated, "But you have to remember, sir, I have only been seeing Mr. Simmons for a short while. Much too short a time for him to trust me enough to allow me to be around when he's dealing with his business associates."

"I agree!" the agent in charge stated. "But I'm going to need you to be on top of this, Agent Washington. The both of you. Are we understood, Agent Thomas?"

"Yes, sir!" Jennifer replied as she held back from laughing after seeing Mia sarcastically roll her eyes.

After hanging up with their boss, Jennifer wasted

no time asking Mia what was wrong with her.

"I'm fine!" Mia answered as she began packing up her papers.

"Mia!" Jennifer said, getting her best friend and partner's attention. "What's wrong?"

Mia stared at Jennifer a few moments before she gave in. Mia dropped back into her chair and sighed out loud.

"I think I'm about to lose this really good guy, Jenn."

"What guy, and why am I just now hearing about him?" Jennifer questioned as she sat forward with a grin on her face.

Mia smiled back at Jennifer, the way she always did when her friend was up in her business. Finally, Mia gave in.

"His name's Sean, and he lives in the building I just moved into."

"Tell me more!"

"He's about six foot even with the most gorgeous smoky-gray eyes, and a body that drives me crazy, Jennifer."

"How old is he?"

"He's younger than I am."

"How old, Mia?"

"He's twenty-five!" Mia answered, but quickly said, "But he's turning twenty-six in four months."

"I'll let you deal with that!" Jennifer told her. "So what does he do for a living?"

"He's actually an architect," Mia answered with a smile.

"Well, damn!" Jennifer stated, smiling again. "No

wonder you're overlooking the fact that there's a nine-year difference in age between the two of you. His ass is paid, girl."

"Actually!" Mia began in a tone that instantly got Jennifer's attention. "He doesn't know that I'm thirty-four, and I didn't tell him that I'm with the FBI."

"Jesus, Mia!" Jennifer cried. "You lied to the boy and you're keeping things as important as what you do for a living from him? You must not really see things working with this guy, do you?"

"Actually, I think I'm already falling for him, Jennifer," Mia admitted, but then gave her friend a smile that had Jennifer shaking her head at her.

"What am I gonna do with you, Mia?"

"Help me!" Mia pleaded with a face that showed just how serious she was about her best friend helping her out with fixing what she was sure she was messing up with Sean, before it was too late to fix at all.

~ ~ ~

Sean was really in no mood to be going out, but he was always a man of his word. So he got dressed after his cousin Tony called and told him what time to meet up at his Aunt Toni's house, so they all could ride out to the club together.

Sean had gotten a new haircut and razor edge earlier in the day, and he now stood in front of the mirror brushing his hair that had waves all through it in a 360 style. He was dressed in a Gucci outfit with matching loafers. He then grabbed the specially-made leather Gucci jacket on his bed before walking out of his bedroom.

He locked up his condo and then took the elevator

down to the lobby, since he parked his ride out front. He was just stepping outside when his cell phone went off.

He pulled it out and saw that it was Michael Brown.

"Yeah?" Sean answered.

"Sean, ya busy?"

"Naw! What's up, Detective?"

"I've got another job for you."

"I'm listening."

Sean climbed into his BMW while listening to Michael first give him the name of the new target and then the details about him.

Sean waited until the retired detective was finished and then said, "You got a picture of how this Richard Allen looks?"

"I'm sending it to your phone as soon as we hang

up!" Michael told him. "One more thing. You need to be careful because he's tied in with one of the strongest and deadliest drug lords in Miami and all of Florida. Luther Simmons isn't one to be taken lightly, Sean."

"Okay, $250,000."

"Only $250,000? Why so low this time?"

"Because I've gotta handle something else tonight, but send me that photo."

"I will," Michael told him. "But I'm going to need this done before Monday, so that gives you three days to handle this job."

"Relax, Detective," Sean told him before hanging up the phone.

~ ~ ~

Sean made it to his auntie's house a short time later. Once he arrived, he saw Tony and the rest of the crew there, but also his Aunt Toni and her dude, Marvin, all dressed up with their friends. He then noticed all their rides parked in front of her house.

He parked his BMW behind Tony's SUV and climbed out, just as Tony, Hulk, and T.J. walked up onto his car.

"Damn! What took you so long?" Tony asked as he hugged his cousin. "We been waiting on your ass for thirty minutes now!"

"I had to take care of something," Sean stated, watching as his aunt and Marvin climbed into his DTS followed by all of their people. "We ready to go?" he asked, looking back to Tony.

"Naw, we're still waiting on Nina and her sister Maria," T.J. told Sean. "They took their asses up to the store."

"Naw!" Hulk spoke up as he tapped T.J. on the arm to get his attention and then nodded out toward the street. "Here they come now."

Sean turned his head and looked back behind him to see Nina's Charger pull up. He walked out to the car with the others as the girls climbed out.

"I see you finally decided to show up!" Nina said, shooting Sean a look, but she was very aware of the way his eyes were taking her in with the Yves Saint Laurent body dress she intentionally wore for him.

"Yo, can we get the fuck outta here now before it gets any later?" T.J. went off while walking toward his own car.

Nina cut her eyes back toward Sean and caught him stealing one more look before he walked off. She allowed a small smile as she climbed back into her car ready to leave as well.

~ ~ ~

Mia arrived at the club more than ten cars deep. She rode in the back of a Rolls-Royce Wraith seated beside Luther Simmons, who sat talking on his cell phone in a whispered tone of voice. She sat trying to hear as best she could while playing as if she was bored and was simply staring out of her window waiting until he had finished his phone call.

"I apologize, Tiffany," Luther told Mia after hanging up his phone, just as the car stopped at the front doors of the overly crowded nightclub where he was celebrating his thirty-seventh birthday.

Mia told Luther that she accepted his apology and showed a smile that earned her a kiss to the cheek, just as the back door was opened for them to step out. Mia climbed from the car first to a big team of Luther's security that made a path from the car straight through the huge-as-hell crowd up to the front doors to the nightclub. She knew the exact moment Luther climbed from the car, as the crowd began screaming and yelling out his name.

She allowed Luther to wrap his arm around her waist, and he rested his hand on the top curve of her butt. Mia followed alongside the drug lord into the club as if he owned the place.

~ ~ ~

"Oh hell naw!" Nina cried as soon as she turned up into the parking lot at Club Palace.

She not only noticed the big-ass crowd, but also the caravan of Escalades that was blocking the front entrance to the club. She also peeped the Wraith that was parked among the SUVs.

"That's gotta be Luther Simmons and his people," Jennifer stated as Nina found a place to park her car.

Nina parked once she found an open spot at the far end of the lot. But before she got out, she checked herself one last time in the mirror.

"Damn, baby, what's up with ya?" Nina heard as soon as she climbed from the car.

She turned back over her shoulder to see a crowd of three guys standing beside an F-150 smoking and staring. She simply smiled as she closed and locked up her car, and then walked around to meet Jennifer at the back end of her Charger.

Nina heard the flirtatious whistles from the men behind them, but both girls ignored them as they headed over to where Tony and the others stood waiting for them.

"Nina, you see that?" Jennifer asked her sister as they approached the guys. "Bitch, look at how Sean is looking at you."

"I'm not paying his ass no attention," Nina lied, since she was staring at him just as hard, missing the look of disbelief her sister had shot her.

"Y'all ready?" Tony asked, dropping his arm around Jennifer's shoulder.

"Hell yeah!" Jennifer replied as the group started toward the front entrance of the club.

Tony left the parking lot and walked over to the front doors of the club. He led the group through the crowd and heard his name from a few people that recognized him. He stepped up to the doorman, who slightly recognized him.

"So, you still mad at me?" Sean softly spoke into Nina's ear as Tony spoke with the doorman.

Sean was standing directly behind Nina and breathing softly onto the back of her neck. She closed her eyes for a brief moment and sighed, trying to control herself with how close Sean was up on her. She could smell the cologne he was wearing.

"Ain't shit to be mad about! You made your decision, so what am I mad for?" she replied.

"Nina, you already—!"

"Y'all come on in," Tony called out, interrupting Sean and Nina.

Sean looked from Tony back to Nina as she walked off as though the two of them were just talking. He shook his head and gave up as he followed the others into the club.

~ ~ ~

Sean didn't feel the vibe of the club as soon as he walked inside. He saw how crowded and packed it was. Sean really was not a fan of crowded places, but he followed the others through the club and ended up at the bar.

"Cuz, what's up?" Tony yelled over the crowd and noise to Sean. "What you drinking?"

"Naw, I'm good!" Sean yelled back as he stood looking around the crowd.

"Here!" Tony yelled as he handed Sean the drink he had bought for him.

Sean accepted the drink, but he really didn't pay any attention to what he was taking, since his eyes were focused on the crowd up in the VIP area where he noticed a familiar face.

"Cuz, what's up?" Tony asked, after noticing the expression on Sean's face.

"Nothing!" Sean replied, shifting his gaze from the familiar face to look back at his cousin. "Everything's good, Cousin."

~ ~ ~

Tony enjoyed the night, and they all had a good time together. He actually got Sean out onto the dance floor with a cute-as-hell brown-skinned female that stepped to Sean. Tony was dancing all up on Maria when the commotion broke up the moment.

"Fuck!" Tony said after instantly recognizing the face of the lead of the six-man crowd that was facing off with Hulk and T.J.

Tony then noticed Nina pushing through the crowd trying to get to Hulk and T.J.

Tony took off, with Jennifer behind him, and pushed through the crowd to get to his boys before shit turned real ugly.

"Yo, what's up?" he yelled, getting between T.J. and Hulk. "Fuck is the problem?"

"Muthafucker, you know what the problem is!" Marcus growled. "Don't think I ain't heard about the beef you and my brother Bull was going through, nigga! If I find out you or any one of these weak-ass punk muthafuckers you rolling with had anything to do with my brother's murder—!"

"What?" Nina screamed while pushing right past Tony to get up in Marcus's face. "What the fuck is you gonna do, nigga? Ya best bet is to go on about your business and live since ya punk-ass brother ain't no more!"

"Bitch, what the fuck you say?" Marcus yelled, cocking back to swing at Nina, only to find himself being grabbed right before pain exploded from his forehead after having it slammed down onto the bar top.

"Fuck no!" Sean heard.

He looked up from Marcus to first see one of Marcus's boys rush at him and reach for his waist. He snatched up the beer bottle from the bar top and smashed it across homeboy's face, only to grab the bar stool and sling it into the rest of Marcus's homeboy, directing it at the friend that was also reaching under his shirt.

"The next muthafucker I see reach for anything won't be throwing stools and bottles anymore. I'ma send something ya way neither one of you muthafuckers will be able to get up from. Now y'all can either get your boys up off the floor and get outta here, or we can start turning this shit into a murder scene. What's it gonna be?"

~ ~ ~

Mia could not believe what she was seeing and who was involved. She stood at the rail inside the VIP area beside Luther Simmons while looking down onto the show that was unfolding before them.

"Well handled!" Luther stated, smiling as he watched half of the disturbance turn and leave the club with their wounded. "What do you think, Mr. Allen?"

"Very impressive!" Richard responded, still watching the well-dressed and strongly handsome young man that put on the well-performed show only a brief moment ago. "Maybe I should offer this one a job on my staff."

"You read my mind!" Luther shot back, waving to one of his men to go and get the young man from downstairs and bring him up to their VIP area to meet him.

"This can't be happening!" Mia whispered to herself as she returned to her seat following behind Luther Simmons and his friend Richard Allen.

Mia came up with a quick plan and excused herself from the others. She whispered to Luther that she needed to use the restroom. She then snatched up her purse and walked quickly away from their table in the VIP section.

She spotted Jennifer at the bar and spoke into the microphone she was wearing inside her left ear to get her attention and tell her to immediately meet her in the restroom.

Mia stepped into the ladies' room and waited at the sink until Jennifer burst in. Mia wasted no time explaining the new problem.

"Jennifer, I need your help really bad. You saw that guy that was just in the middle of the commotion that just jumped off?"

"Did I?" Jennifer stated with a smile. "Mia, that guy is absolutely gorgeous."

"That's him!" Mia cried out before she looked around and lowered her voice. "That's Sean, the guy I'm seeing!"

"Oh my God!" Jennifer cried in disbelief. "Mia, he is gorgeous, girl! No wonder you've been lying to that man. I would too!"

"I haven't lied to Sean," Mia stated in defense.

"Forget all of that. I have a bigger problem, Jennifer. Luther just saw Sean in that fight, and now he wants to offer him a job."

"Holy shit!"

"My feelings exactly!" Mia returned. "Listen, I've got a plan, but I need to get a message to Sean. I want you to catch Sean and explain to him that I really need to talk and that it's extremely important. Let him know that I love him, Jennifer. Please!"

~ ~ ~

Mia returned to the VIP area a few minutes later and took a deep breath before walking back up the stairs. As she headed upstairs she could hear Luther's voice, but she quickly spotted Sean's familiar strong and muscular back even inside the leather jacket he was wearing.

"She's back!" Luther spoke up after noticing his date had returned. "Mr. Carter, I would like you to meet my girlfriend, Miss Tiffany Moore."

Mia met Sean's eyes as soon as she sat down, and caught the brief look of surprise that appeared on his face before it quickly turned into anger before all expression was completely gone.

"Miss Moore," Sean respectfully answered, holding out his hand and gently shaking it. "It's good to meet you."

"Likewise, Mr. Carter," Mia replied as she tried holding Sean's eyes, only for him to easily turn his attention back to Luther Simmons.

~ ~ ~

Sean finished up his conversation with Luther Simmons and Richard Allen after declining both offers from the two of them to work on their security staff. He then walked out of the VIP section without a backward glance, but he was fully aware of Mia's eyes burning a hole into the back of his head.

His mind was already made up of how to deal with his target that just so happened to be in the same place as him. Sean made it a few feet from the stairs when he felt someone grab his arm.

"Whoa!" Jennifer cried, throwing up her hands and recognizing the movement that Sean jerked back to make.

"Relax, handsome! I'm a friend, Sean.'"

Sean immediately caught the use of his name and turned to face the white, green-eyed woman.

"Explain to me how it is that you know name, and who exactly are you?"

"Can we go outside and talk?" Jennifer asked, watching Sean slightly nod his head before motioning for her to lead the way.

SEVEN

S ean followed Jennifer out of the nightclub and into the parking lot. She walked over to the Nissan Altima and hit the locks by key remote. Jennifer then motioned for Sean to climb into the car as she opened the driver's door and climbed inside herself.

"All right, I'm listening!" Sean stated as he sat inside the passenger seat and stared straight ahead, still fully aware of the woman next to him.

"Okay," Jennifer began, taking a deep breath before continuing. "I'll be truthful with you, Sean. I've only just heard about you today, but the person who told me about you is someone that really cares deeply for you and wants you to know that she loves you."

"You still haven't answered my question yet," Sean

stated in a calm yet graveyard-serious tone of voice.

"Okay," Jennifer replied. "My name is Jennifer Thomas, and I'm friends with Mia. She asked me to—!"

"I've heard enough!" Sean answered, cutting Jennifer off as he attempted to climb back out of the car, only to have Jennifer grab his arm again to stop him.

"Sean, wait!" she pleaded with him. "At least hear me out before you just leave. Please!"

Sean looked back over at Jennifer and met her eyes. He sighed deeply as he sat back into his seat and shut the car door.

"I'm listening, but this better be worth my time."

Jennifer made the decision right then and said, "Okay, Sean. I know you think that Mia lied to you, but she's just trying to keep you safe. That guy she's in the club with isn't really her boyfriend, but his business is—!"

"Drugs!" Sean interrupted. "I know all about Luther Simmons; and before you continue, I know all about Mia being FBI as well. But what I don't know is why the hell my woman is at the club on a date with Luther Simmons. Can you answer that for me, Jennifer?"

Jennifer was caught completely by surprise after what Sean just told her.

She sat staring at him a moment in shock before saying, "You're not really an architect, are you?"

Sean slowly smiled as he looked back over at Jennifer.

"We all have our secrets, don't we?"

~ ~ ~

"Mr. Carter," Luther Simmons cried out in surprise after seeing Sean walk back into the VIP area, only just leaving a short while ago. "You're back!"

Mia was surprised as she stared up at Sean in wonder. She sat and listened to him as he changed his decision and now agreed to work for Luther. She had to catch herself before going off hearing Jennifer through her microphone telling her to calm down.

"So you've changed your mind, Mr. Carter?" Luther asked. "What brought about this change?"

"Let's just say I thought about the offer and I want in!" Sean told him. "Now, let's talk about my fee."

"How does $60,000 every two weeks sound?" Luther asked with a smile.

"Not gonna work!" Sean replied, surprising Luther

and causing Richard Allen to chuckle. "My price is $100,000 every two weeks!"

"What, $100,000 every two weeks, you say, huh?" Luther repeated, laughing lightly. "And why would I pay you that type of money, Mr. Carter?"

"Let's just say that I'll be the one to keep you out of jail and snitches away from you as well. Ain't that right, Mr. Allen?"

Richard was completely caught off guard after what was just announced.

He immediately shot to his feet and said, "What the hell are you implying? Are you calling me the police?"

"I'm not calling you shit!" Sean said with the same calm voice he always used. "I'm telling you that you're the police working with Miami PD against Mr. Simmons. Are you not working with Detective Cook and Sergeant Wright on investigating Luther Simmons?"

"This is insane!" Richard yelled as he shot Luther a look. "Are you gonna just sit there and listen to this? Say something?"

"Have a seat, Richard!" Luther told him as he dug out his own cell phone. "I will figure this out in moments."

"This is bullshit!" Richard shouted as he grabbed his jacket and started toward the exit, only for Sean to swiftly step into his path and block his way. "Get the hell outta my way!" Richard yelled, making the mistake of taking a swing at Sean, only to find himself spun around and then suddenly slammed face-down on the VIP table directly in front of Luther.

~ ~ ~

"How did you know Allen was working with the police?" Luther asked Sean as the two of them sat in the back of his Rolls-Royce.

"At first, I didn't really recognize him without the facial hair, but the name sounded real familiar," Sean explained. "I used to do bodyguard work for a guy back down south by the name of Sammie Tillmen. You recognize the name?"

"Tillmen and I've done good business together in the past!" Luther admitted.

"Well, Allen's the reason he was sentenced to life in federal prison," Sean told the drug lord. "I guess you're lucky we crossed paths tonight, huh?"

"I was just thinking the same exact thing, my friend," Luther stated, just as a tap came from the passenger side window right before the door opened and his head of security stuck his head inside the car.

"Boss, we all ready?" Frank told Luther while ignoring Sean altogether.

Luther nodded his head in response to his head of security, and then dug out a business card from his coat pocket and handed it to Sean.

"You work for me now. Call this number first thing in the morning at 5:00 a.m. Are we clear?"

"5:00 a.m.," Sean repeated before taking the card and climbing out of the car.

Luther watched his new bodyguard walk off, and then he watched his friend Frank climb his ex-linebacker body into the car.

"Did you take care of Miss Moore, Frank?"

"She's on her way home now inside a taxi, boss," Frank answered as the Rolls-Royce pulled off.

~ ~ ~

Sean watched the Rolls-Royce and its caravan of Escalades leave the parking lot of the nightclub. Sean got into his car, and before he could even start it up, his passenger door was snatched open and Mia climbed inside.

"Who the hell are you?" she yelled at him, slamming the car door shut.

Sean said nothing at first. He got the car started and then pulled out of the parking lot.

"So, when did you plan on telling me I was dating an FBI agent, Mia? Or should I call you Tiffany Moore?"

"Okay, Sean, I'm sorry. I should have told you the truth, but how do I tell my boyfriend that I'm with the FBI?" she said with a loud sigh.

"You just did!"

"And you would have accepted it?"

"Am I now?"

Sean shook his head as Mia stared at him.

"Who are you, Sean?" she repeated her question.

"That's not the question you should be asking me," he told her. "The question you should be asking is what am I?"

"Excuse me?" Mia said, confused. "What the hell does that mean, Sean?"

Sean shook his head and smiled as he began pulling over into the far right lane to turn into a Denny's restaurant. At the same time, he spotted Jennifer's Nissan Altima trailing behind them.

He parked the BMW and watched as Jennifer turned into the parking lot and pulled up beside them.

Sean let down Mia's window and saw Jennifer do the same.

"You may as well get in with us."

Sean waited until Jennifer shut off her Altima and then climbed in the back seat of his ride. He let Mia's window back up and then looked back to her.

"So what's going on between you two and Luther Simmons?"

"Sean, I can't tell you that!" Mia admitted. "That's FBI information only."

Sean nodded his head.

"So you want me to trust you with information that can send me possibly to death row, but you can't tell me what type of investigation you two got building on Luther Simmons."

"Sean, this is—!"

"We're investigating large amounts of heroin that've been finding their way over here into the state, Sean," Jennifer told him truthfully. "Just recently, two known drug dealers were arrested and caught with the same heroin we're investigating, and it had Luther Simmons's trademark label on each of the packages. Also, there were the murders of two detectives not far away from one of Luther Simmons's areas, and we have reason to believe that both of them were murdered by Luther and his men."

"What makes you so sure of that?" Sean asked, looking from Jennifer to Mia and back to Jennifer, only for Mia to answer.

"Because both detectives were investigating Luther Simmons, Sean. Now they're both dead, and the murders were just swept up under the rug and forgotten about."

"How long ago was this?" Sean asked next.

"Almost two months now!" Mia answered, but then switched things up. "Now how about explaining who you are and how it is that you know about Richard Allen working with the Miami PD against Luther Simmons."

Mia sighed loudly as Sean ran his hand over his face before meeting her eyes again.

"Do either of you know what a mercenary is?"

EIGHT

Sean was up at 4:00 a.m. the next morning and getting in a long and hard workout for which he was overdue. He then showered and dressed by 4:55 and was on the phone by exactly 5:00 a.m., as was told to him after he called the number on the business card given to him by Luther Simmons.

Sean spoke with a woman who was expecting his call, only to be given an address to report to by 6:15 a.m. Sean grabbed his jacket and keys and headed for his door, only to hear his cell phone begin to ring through his Bluetooth in his right ear.

"Yeah!"

"Where are you, Sean?"

Sean recognized Mia's voice and answered, "I'm on

my way to some address that Simmons's peoples gave me."

"What's the address?"

"Mia!"

"Sean, this isn't a game. What's the address?"

Sean made a decision and gave Mia the address to the diner where he had met Michael Brown. He also made up a time to meet her.

Sean left his apartment building and found the real address he was given by the woman on the phone. He found that it was some type of warehouse. He parked his BMW in front of the warehouse entrance, shut off the car, and climbed out just as the warehouse entrance doors were being pushed open.

"You're early," Luther stated with a smile at the sight of Sean. He waved him inside the warehouse. "I like to see a man that's always on time. Was the rest of your night good, Sean?"

"Always!" Sean replied, looking over at the back entrance where Luther's head of security stood staring at something.

"Come on!" Luther told him upon seeing the direction in which Sean was staring.

Sean followed alongside the drug lord. While walking over to the head of security, Sean could hear grunts and what sounded like muffled screams. He stepped outside behind Luther to see three young muscular guys outside. One was going to work on an almost unrecognizable Richard Allen.

"You remember our friend, Richard, right?" Luther asked, smiling over at Sean before continuing. "Well, I've been able to get a lot of information out of our friend, but now there's just one thing left to be taken care of."

Sean looked down at the gun that was held out in front of him by the head of security.

Sean looked over at Luther and laughed before saying, "I got my own."

He pulled out his Glock .40 from his back holster and stepped toward Richard Allen's beaten body. Sean thought nothing of it as he put a bullet into Richard's head.

Boom!

Sean turned back around to face Luther Simons, who stood smiling. He slid his burner back into his holster said, "Any more tests you got for me?"

"Not at all!" Luther replied while still smiling.

"Let's go do some shopping, Mr. Carter."

~ ~ ~

Mia was growing more and more upset the longer she and Jennifer sat in the parking lot outside the diner, where Sean had told them they would meet.

"I can't believe this shit!" Mia yelled, slamming her phone shut and really wanting to throw the thing.

She then took a deep breath and tried to calm herself down.

"I take it Sean gave us some bullshit information and address?" Jennifer asked, staring over at her pissed-off partner and friend.

"I don't know how I let myself fall for his lying!" Mia began before she snatched up her ringing cell phone and saw Sean's name on the screen. "Sean, where in the hell are you?"

"I'm right behind you."

Mia heard the line die right after what Sean had told her. She looked back and expected to see him, only to see a pearl-black and chrome-edged Porsche Panamera turning into the parking lot.

"Where the hell is this boy?"

"Ummm, Mia," Jennifer said, getting Mia's attention and pointing out the passenger window. "Girl, look who it is!"

Mia turned her head to see what Jennifer was talking about and found herself staring at Sean seated behind the wheel of the same Porsche Panamera that had just pulled into the parking lot.

"What in the hell?" she cried as she climbed from the Altima just as Sean was also climbing from the Porsche. "Boy, where the hell did you get his from?"

Sean returned Mia's hug and then accepted the kiss

she gave him.

He looked up just as Jennifer jokingly said, "I guess she ain't mad at you no more for lying about the meeting place."

"I forgot about that!" Mia cried, turning around and punching Sean in the chest. "Why'd you have me drive way out here, and you knew this wasn't the meeting place, Sean?"

"Mia, you said it yourself, this isn't a game and I don't trust Luther Simmons," Sean reminded her. "I really didn't want you there just in case things weren't what they were supposed to be."

"So what did happen?" Jennifer spoke up.

Sean explained to both of them about the meeting with Luther at the warehouse, but he left out the part about killing Richard Allen. He continued telling them that Luther took him shopping for new clothes as well as the car that he was now driving.

"So Luther bought you the car, huh?" Mia asked, looking the car over and even peeping inside the driver's window. "I'll be honest and admit that the car does match you and your style, Sean. I like it for you."

"I kind of like it myself," Sean replied, looking over at the Porsche before changing the conversation. "All right, listen. I'm going to tell you everything that I find out about this guy, but the both of you have to keep me informed on what moves the two of you are going to make, or the deal is off. What's it gonna be?"

"Sean, you know the FBI isn't going to allow us to give away their plans to you," Jennifer told him.

"Who gives a fuck about the FBI, Jennifer?" Sean stated. "I'm making sure you two are safe. I could care less about what the FBI is planning to do. If something is going down and you two are involved, then I want to know about it. I'm not changing my mind on this, so what's it gonna be?"

Mia looked from Sean and met Jennifer's eyes. Mia then made an expression that was like asking her partner what she thought.

"Okay, Sean," Jennifer said, looking back at him. "We'll do this your way from now on, but you have to be completely honest with us from now on. Do we have a deal?"

Sean slowly smiled at both women.

"Do whatever it is you all need to do, because Luther's leaving to meet with what he's calling a potential new client. But he's also having a meeting with another client that owes him payment from a shipment he received, so things may get a little outta hand."

"Why does it sound like you're looking forward to things getting out of hand, Sean?" Jennifer asked with a smile on her face.

Sean winked his eye at her and smirked.

He then turned his attention to Mia and asked, "What you about to do?"

"Why?" she asked him.

"Because I want you to come with me and meet someone," he told her as he was opening the driver's door to the Porsche.

Mia shook her head and smiled at Sean. She then told Jennifer that she would call her later as she jogged around to the passenger side of the Porsche.

~ ~ ~

Sean and Mia spent more time than necessary just driving around together and talking before he finally pulled up in front of a house. Sean parked the Porsche behind the Mercedes-Benz truck, and they both climbed out of the car.

"Whose house is this, Sean?" Mia asked as the two of them crossed the lawn.

"You'll see!" he replied, smiling as he glanced over at Mia.

He rang the doorbell once the two of them were both on the porch. Sean looked back and caught Mia looking around the neighborhood just as the front door opened.

"Sean!"

Hearing the female voice screaming her man's name, Mia turned her full attention onto Sean and saw a young teenage female all over him. Mia stared and waited until the girl released him.

"Mia, this is who I want you to meet," he told her with a smile. "This is my sister, Tasha."

"Sister?" Mia repeated, feeling really stupid. "Tasha, it's good to finally meet you. Sean talks about you a lot."

"He's told me about you too," Tasha admitted. "He didn't tell me you looked like that lady from that movie *Love Jones* though.

"You're talking about Nia Long," Mia said with a smile. "I've heard that so many times that I'm beginning to believe it myself now."

After they entered the house after the greeting was finished, Sean led Mia by the hand while following Tasha through the house and into the kitchen, where they found Tracy.

"Momma," Tasha cried out, "Sean's here, and he brought his girlfriend, Mia."

Tracy smiled as she walked over to hug her stepson, and received a kiss on her cheek in return.

She then turned to Mia and said, "So you're Mia? Sean keeps telling us about you, and he finally brought you over to meet us."

"I've heard a lot about you and Tasha as well," Mia admitted. "I had no idea he was bringing me here to meet you all today, however."

"Are you two hungry?" Tracy asked as she turned back around toward the stove.

"Yes!" Sean quickly answered.

"I'm fine," Mia replied.

"She's eating, Tracy," Sean quickly added.

NINE

Sean flew out to San Antonio and met with Donavon Williams, who was a potential client with whom Luther Simmons was considering doing business. Sean did his job silently and stayed close to Luther while keeping an open eye on everything around them. Frank and six other members of the security team were brought along as well.

After taking care of business and seeing Luther and Donavon shake hands, Sean learned everything he needed to know. He then escorted Luther back outside to the rental Bentley Continental.

"I love when good business is handled correctly," Luther said aloud with a smile. He then called up front to Frank and said, "Let's go meet with our friend, Paul

O'Deil, Frank."

After Luther gave Frank directions to their next stop, Luther gave Sean his instructions.

"I want you to keep a real close eye out when we walk up into this place, Sean. We're not on our home turf anymore; so that means if anybody so much as blinks too many times, I want whatever was on their minds made known to us. We understand each other, Sean?"

"Perfectly clear!" Sean answered with a small smile.

Sean and Luther made the trip across town, which was about fifteen minutes from where the meeting was held with Donavon Williams. The two men then stared out the back window of the Bentley until they pulled up to the restaurant.

Once the car was parked and the back door was

opened by Frank, Sean was the first to step out of the Bentley. He was followed a few moments later by Luther Simmons.

Luther glanced around and felt the eyes he knew were watching him. He then whispered something to Sean, who then nodded, turned around, and walked off, leaving the group.

"Let's go, Frank," Luther ordered his head of security as they entered the restaurant with his team surrounding him with Frank in the lead.

~ ~ ~

"Where the hell is Sean going?" Mia heard Jennifer ask, which was the same question she had just asked herself in her head.

Mia wanted to get out and follow him, but she quickly lost sight of Sean after he stepped in front of an SUV that was parked at the end of the street. Mia began looking everywhere for signs of him, only to see that Sean had disappeared.

"What the hell!"

~ ~ ~

"Paul!" Luther yelled out as he entered the room he was just told he was not allowed to enter by the two armed men who were now knocked out on the other side of the door.

Paul heard his name being called just as the door opened. He then looked up from the money that he and this three trusted workers were counting out, only to see Luther Simmons standing a few feet in front of him.

"What the hell? How in the fuck did you get in here?"

"Through the door, Paul," Luther answered sarcastically as he walked up to the table and picked up a stack of bills with a big smile on his face as he ran his thumb through them. "Is this for me, Paul?"

"What the hell are you doing here, Simmons?" Paul asked as his anger built. "Our business ended long ago. We have nothing else to discuss. Why are you here?"

"That's just it, Paul," Luther began, pulling out one of the open chairs at the table where Paul and his men were seated. He then tossed the money back onto the table. "I see things differently. I remember it very differently, since you still owe me $3 million from the last shipment you got from me."

Paul laughed as he secretly pressed the emergency button that was beneath the table, and then sat back in his seat.

J.L. ROSE & J.L. TURNER

"I remember none of the bullshit you're talking about. How I see it, you've made your last trip out here disrespecting me, Simmons," Mr. O'Deil said with a cocky smile.

Luther heard the door open behind him and watched Paul's facial expression change as a team of six men were escorted into the room with their hands on top of their heads. They were all made to kneel beside Luther on his left as Sean stepped up beside him on his right. Luther slowly began to laugh while watching the cockiness fade from Paul's face and be replaced first by shock and then by fear.

"Were you expecting them, Paul?" Luther asked, nodding over to his left at the six kneeling men. "I remember the two from the roof you kept there for protection just in case, but the other four must be new."

Luther laughed even more as he sat watching Paul and saw the direction the so-called drug lord was looking.

"I see you've taken an interest in my new friend. Allow me to introduce my new bodyguard, Paul."

Luther stood up from his seat and ignored all of Paul's men as he made his way around the table to stand beside Paul.

"I intended to kill you when I got here, Paul, but then I would be missing out on my money. So here's the thing, Paul, you have two days to have my $3 million, or I will be sending my new friend back to see about you, Paul. Do we understand each other, Paul?"

"I'll have your money, Mr. Simmons!" Paul answered with respect now, nodding his head up and

J.L. ROSE & J.L. TURNER

down.

Luther laughed as he shook his head sadly at Paul. He then started for the door and motioned for Sean to follow him out.

Once outside the room and leaving a scared shitless Paul O'Deil inside with his men, Luther suddenly stopped at the entrance to the restaurant in front, which caused his entire team to stop immediately behind him.

"Sean!" he called out.

"Yeah!" Sean answered, sliding up beside him.

"I've changed my mind," Luther stated as he looked over to meet Sean's gray eyes. "Kill Mr. O'Deil for me, please."

Nothing else needed to be said. Sean turned and started back toward the back of the restaurant while ignoring the stares he was receiving from the employees.

~ ~ ~

Paul was completely pissed off after being totally disrespected in his own establishment. He then yelled out in anger and slapped at the money that was covering the table, sending it flying up into the air.

"I'm sick of this cock-sucking bastard Luther Simmons. I want his ass dead!" Paul screamed out loud as he shot up out of his seat at the same time the secret backroom door flew open. Paul's eyes flew open wide as saucers once they locked on Luther Simmons's personal bodyguard. "Whh, what do you want?"

"Luther changed his mind," Sean said. He swiftly pulled the Glock .40 from his back holster and did as he was told and killed Paul O'Deil.

He also bodied all of Paul's men before calmly turning and walking back out of the room.

~ ~ ~

Sean made the flight back to Miami after all the business was handled in San Antonio. Sean rode with Luther back to his mansion in Boca Raton, and hung out with his employer talking about business at first, before moving on to friendly conversation.

"So, Sean, what is it you do for fun?" Luther asked him. "You seeing anybody?"

"Why?"

"Why?" Luther repeated confused.

"Why do I need to have any type of relationship when all it does is tie you down to someone? I'm married to my work, and I fuck whenever my dick gets hard, so what more do I need?"

Luther softly chuckled and then patted Sean on the back.

"I want you to relax a little bit, Sean. Matter of fact, I've got something planned for this Friday night for Tiffany, since I've been ignoring her lately. I want you to bring a date along. It's just going to be the four of us for four days. We'll come back on Tuesday. What do you say?"

"Why do I feel like you're more telling me than asking me?" Sean asked him.

Luther laughed at Sean's question. He then slapped him on the back and said, "I knew I liked you for a reason. You catch on real swiftly."

~ ~ ~

Sean left Luther's mansion a short while later and drove straight to the airport since it was about time for

Mia and Jennifer's plane to land. He turned into the Miami International Airport and easily found a parking spot.

After leaving the lot and walking into the airport lobby, Sean walked over to the food and gift shop to buy something for Mia and Jennifer as well as something for himself to eat since he had not eaten all day.

~ ~ ~

After exiting the plane and walking with the crowd out onto the lobby floor at the airport, Mia and Jennifer wasted no time getting away from the crowd as Mia quickly got on her phone and called Sean.

"What the—?" Mia said after being sent straight to his voice mailbox.

"What happened?" Jennifer asked as the two of

them stood by the bank of pay phones.

"I think Sean's phone is cut off," Mia explained while trying to call him again.

"Maybe he's still with Simmons?"

"He told me he would be here waiting on us once we got in, Jennifer."

"And I am!" Mia and Jennifer heard someone to their left speak up.

The two women watched as Sean walked up to them carrying a mid-sized and a small teddy bear.

"Hey, you!" Sean said as he walked up to Mia.

He stopped directly in front of her. He was so close that her perky C-cup titties were pressed up against his chest. She smiled and stared up into his eyes.

"Hi!" Mia got out in a small voice that was almost a whisper.

Sean bent down and lowered his lips until they were lightly touching Mia's lips. He started off gently and so slowly kissing her, only for the kiss to turn quickly into a strong and deeper kiss from which anyone could tell how much the two wanted each other.

"Umm, excuse me, you two!" Jennifer interrupted, smiling happily for her best friend and Sean. "But have you two forgotten that we're in the middle of the airport and people are watching?"

"Let's get outta here," Sean suggested while still staring down into Mia's hazel-brown eyes.

~ ~ ~

Once they were inside his Porsche and driving away from the airport, Sean went straight into the story about the whole business deal with Donavon Williams as well as the issue with Paul O'Deil, leaving out the part that one of them was killed.

"So, Donavon Williams is working with Luther Simmons now, right?" Mia asked.

She didn't bother with questioning Sean about the whole issue with O'Deil. She decided to bring up his murder with the overall Luther Simmons case once the time was right.

"I'm not sure yet when the whole deal is going down, but I'll let you know when I find out. But I also got a little more news for you, Mia."

"Me?" she asked, staring oddly at Sean. "What news do you have for me, Sean?"

"Well," he slowly began with a smile as he cut his eyes over toward her. "It seems like Luther feels bad about ignoring you these past few days, so he's taking you away somewhere."

"Wait!" she cried out. "What do you mean he's taking me away? Where to?"

"He didn't say yet," Sean admitted. "By the way, he wants me to come along and said I've gotta bring a date."

"A what?" Mia yelled, causing Sean to burst out laughing. "Oh, you think it's funny, huh? And just who the hell are you planning on asking out with you, Sean Carter?"

"Well, I had this one cute woman I've been getting to know lately," Sean joked, when Mia punched him in the arm.

"Boy, do not play with me!" Mia told him in a warning tone.

Sean looked at the rearview mirror back at a

smiling Jennifer who sat listening to them.

"What's up, Jennifer? You gonna let me take you out, cutie?"

Jennifer was caught completely off guard by Sean's question. She shifted her gaze over toward Mia and saw the look on her best friend's face. She was already certain that Mia really did not like the idea at all.

~ ~ ~

Sean dropped Jennifer off at her apartment and drove straight to his and Mia's apartment building. Both of them rode the elevator up past her floor and got off at Sean's floor together. Sean unlocked and then opened his condo door and allowed Mia inside first. He followed her inside, closing and locking the door behind him, only to turn back around and have Mia attack him by wrapping her arms up around his neck as she began kissing him.

"Take me to your bedroom!" Mia insisted, breaking their kiss long enough to get her words out.

Sean gently picked up Mia by the butt as she wrapped her legs around his waist. Sean carried her back to his bedroom, kicked the door shut behind him, and then walked over to the bed and gently laid her on the mattress.

"Please tell me you've got a condom, Sean," Mia said in a hopeful tone, staring up at him.

"Top drawer, left-hand side night table," he answered as he was pulling off his jacket.

Mia was smiling now as she retrieved the condom box from the night table dresser drawer. She turned around and froze once her eyes found and stuck onto Sean's hard and muscular, toned, and extremely defined, cut body.

"You plan on getting with the program, or do you plan on just staring?" Sean asked, smiling down at Mia in only his boxer shorts.

"Umm, yeah!" Mia got out, shaking off her daze-like state to begin undressing.

~ ~ ~

"Oh my God!"

Crying out to God each time Sean pushed up into her with the blessing that God himself gave to the boy, Mia dug her nails into his back once he sat up onto his arms and began pushing even deeper than she thought she was able to take inside of her.

"Sean!" she cried out. "Baby, you're too deep! Oh God, Sean! Baby, you're going to make me! Oh my God!"

Mia tried her hardest to take what he was giving and really enjoy it all, but she was worried about how deep he was inside of her. She quickly wrapped her arms back around him and held on tight as Sean began slow and deep stroking her just right, hitting the spot she did not even know she had.

"Come for me!" Sean told her, whispering directly into her ear.

"Baby, I feel it!" Mia cried out, pushing back against Sean as he also began pushing faster.

She could feel him losing control a little and letting her know he was also close to cumming.

Mia closed and squeezed her eyes shut just as the build-up reached its highest point and she heard Sean growl.

"Shit, Mia! Baby, I'm cumming!"

Mia then exploded at the same point, screaming out Sean's name all while she was cumming as well.

~ ~ ~

Mia was unsure exactly when she fell asleep or how long she had even been asleep, but she quickly realized first that she was not in her own bed. She remembered that she was actually still in Sean's bed, which caused her to smile, only to quickly notice that he was not in the bed next to her.

She sat up in the bed and looked around the bedroom, which was empty of Sean. Even the master bathroom door was wide open. Mia pushed back the blanket that she didn't remember crawling underneath. She then climbed naked from the bed, but picked up her panties and put on one of Sean's T-shirts. She then left the bedroom in search of Sean.

She made her way through his condo and then heard sounds coming from behind a closed door that was two doors down from his bedroom. Mia stopped at the door and placed her ear up against it to hear what sounded like deep breathing and a few grunts coming from inside the room.

She gently and slowly opened the closed door and stuck her head inside, where she saw Sean. She noticed that he was in deep focus while practicing some type of fighting style that she had not seen before.

Mia was so drawn into watching Sean that she boldly stepped into the room and took up position against the wall to continue watching him as he trained. She jumped in surprise when he spun to face her.

"Can't sleep?" he asked.

"Ummmm, I woke up and you weren't there," she

admitted, but then asked, "What was that style you were just using? I didn't recognize it."

"You know martial arts?" he asked, motioning Mia over.

"I took up karate back when I was younger," she proudly told Sean as she stopped directly in front of him.

"Karate, huh?" Sean repeated with a little smirk. "Well, the style you saw me doing is really supposed to be jujitsu, but I've been training myself in mixing both jujitsu and tai chi together."

"You know both?"

"Actually, I know five different styles, Mia. Come on and I'll show you a little tai chi. It's used as a relaxation method as well."

Mia followed Sean's lead and allowed him to show

her the correct techniques of tai chi. Mia tried focusing on what he was teaching her, but she soon found herself focusing only on the smooth way his body moved up against her from the back, causing thoughts of their love-making to return to her mind.

Mia moved before she realized it, and spun inside his arms and faced Sean. She went up onto her toes to kiss him as she wrapped her arms around his neck.

"Let's go back to bed!" she told him, breaking the kiss long enough to tell Sean her request.

She then felt his strong hands grip her butt and gently but easily pick her up from her feet. This allowed her to wrap her legs back around his waist as he carried her back to his bedroom.

TEN

Mia saw that Sean was deep in sleep, especially after getting up at four the morning and dressing. So she wrote him a quick note and explained why she had to leave quietly from his bedroom and let herself out of his apartment. She slid his key back under the door before heading to the elevator.

She took the elevator back down to her own floor and got off with her cell phone in hand. She then called Jennifer as she headed up the hall toward her own place.

"Hello!"

"Jennifer, wake up. It's me, Mia!"

"I know who it is. What do you want is what I don't know, Mia."

"Jennifer, listen," Mia told her as she was locking back up her apartment door once she got it open. "I was thinking about this whole thing with us going out with Luther and Sean. I think it's a good idea because it gives us time to work and find out what we can about Luther."

"Is Sean okay with this?"

"I haven't spoken with him yet about my decision, but I'm sure he'll be okay with it."

"Where are you now?"

"I'm at my apartment, why?"

"Well, I was just wondering since I tried calling you twice earlier and you never answered. I assumed you were still with Sean. So were you?"

"What are you asking me really, Jennifer?"

"Mia, do not play with me! You know damn well

what I really want to know!"

Mia smiled as she got the shower ready to get inside and relax.

She sighed as she said, "Look, I will tell you this. Sean doesn't move or handle himself like a twenty-five-year-old in the bedroom. Trust me!"

"Ohhh, girl!" Jennifer cried out loud, laughing after getting Mia's indirect answer.

Mia laughed as she hung up the phone. She then set down her phone on top of the sink and began undressing to get into the shower.

~ ~ ~

Sean woke up from the ringing of his cell phone. He blindly reached over to the night table and found his phone after a few moments. He answered in the middle of another ring.

"Yeah!"

"Sean!"

"Who this?" he asked half asleep and still not recognizing the voice.

"Sean, this is Jennifer! Wake up, please."

"Jennifer, what's up?" Sean asked, now recognizing Nina's sister's voice. "What's going on?"

He listened as Jennifer quickly went into the story of how Tony and T.J. were caught up in the middle of a drive-by and were shot up pretty badly. Sean was sitting straight up inside his bed fully awake as she continued explaining how after his cousin and T.J. were taken to the hospital and barely seen, they were quickly arrested and taken to jail.

"Where are they, Jennifer?" Sean asked, already out of the bed and getting dressed.

"We think they took them out to the main jail," she explained. "I'm on my way out there now with Toni and Marvin. Nina and Hulk are already there now."

Sean let Jennifer know he was on his way. He then hung up the phone and quickly slipped the black wife beater on over his head before snatching up his blazer-style, black-and-white Miami Heat leather jacket.

~ ~ ~

Sean left his apartment building and flew across town; he could care less about the police or being pulled over for speeding. He made it to the county jail in less time than it took the normal person. He then parked the car illegally, jumped out, jogged across the street, and headed toward the front entrance. He spotted his auntie as soon as he snatched open the door, and heard her going the hell off.

"Sean!" Nina cried, spotting him as soon as he stepped into the lobby. She shot out of her seat and rushed toward him.

"What's going on? What did they say Tony and T.J. were arrested for?"

"They're not saying shit!" Toni yelled from over at the front desk while shooting the guy behind the desk a nasty look.

"Hold on!" Sean said, breaking away from Nina, Jennifer, and Hulk as he walked over to stand with his aunt. He then addressed the officer behind the desk. "I'm going to ask this as respectfully as I can."

"Like I told the lady, man," the officer replied, cutting Sean off, "I can't tell you anything because I don't know anything."

Sean continued, "I want to know what my cousin

and friend were arrested for; and if you don't know, then you need to find out some type of way or I can find out myself. What's it gonna be?"

"Look, man, I already told you-!"

Sean punched the guy straight in the mouth and cut his ass off. The blow sent him flying backward out of his chair, which caused a huge scene in the middle of the jail.

"I'ma see y'all later," Sean told his auntie after seeing more guards and officers rushing to assist their coworker. He cut his eyes over to see both Nina and Maria smiling as they stood with Hulk and Marvin, whom he never saw enter the lobby.

~ ~ ~

After being arrested inside the lobby on assault charges, Sean was taken to a floor and jail unit on which he quickly found out that neither Tony nor T.J. were on. He just as quickly was taken off the unit after breaking the nose of another inmate that stood mean-mugging him.

Three different units and six different beat-up inmates later, Sean landed on the right unit and saw T.J. seated at a table in the back of the dayroom talking with a group of six guys with his right arm in a sling.

"What's good, family?" Sean said as he walked up to the table that T.J. was seated at with the group of guys.

"Oh shit!" T.J. yelled after seeing Sean.

He quickly got up out of his seat and smiled as he and Sean embraced as comfortably as he could with his messed-up arm.

"What the fuck is you doing up in here?"

"I rented a room!" Sean stated sarcastically before he looked around and continued. "Where is Tony at?"

"They just took him to see the nurse," T.J. answered.

"Yo, T.J., who's homeboy?" one of the guys in the room spoke up.

"Yo, this is my brother right here!" T.J. proudly told his boys with a big smile.

T.J. then turned his attention back to Sean and learned that he had found out about him and Tony getting hit up while making a drop and pick-up from Jennifer. T.J. went into more detail and told Sean who he saw that was part of the hit team that tried taking him and Tony out.

"So this Menace guy. Who does he work for?" Sean asked once T.J. was finished explaining.

"He works for himself," one of T.J.'s boys spoke up, letting Sean know. "Dude's one of them murder-for-hire type of niggas."

"Murder for hire, huh?" Sean repeated, smirking at the thought that came to mind. He started to say more when T.J. tapped him on the arm and said, "Here comes Tony now, fam."

Sean turned around and spotted his cousin entering the unit also wearing a sling but walking with the help of a crutch under his left arm. Sean walked over to help his cousin.

"What the—!" Tony started, but paused once he saw who was helping him. "What the hell are you doing up in here?"

"Getting you out!" Sean replied as he got his cousin over to the table where T.J. and the others were waiting. "I got somebody that's gonna get y'all out, but I need to know where I can find this clown at they call Menace."

"That's easy!" another one of T.J.'s boys spoke up. "He chills out there in Murder Grove. He got a bitch out there he chills with."

"What's the female's name?" Sean asked him.

"Monica," he answered. "I think she stays in a green-and-black house that's the third house from the corner."

Sean nodded his head, taking in everything that was told to him. He then looked back at Tony and said, "Write down the names of your boys at the table with you and T.J. now. I'ma see what I can do to get all of y'all outta this shit!"

~ ~ ~

Mia hooked up with Jennifer and they got in contact with their boss to give him an update on how the case was going, both holding back on the information about Paul O'Deil for now. Mia did mention about the possibility of bringing Jennifer onto the case and out into the open if Luther Simmons went along with taking her out on a trip that he was planning for her.

After getting their boss's approval on the whole idea of Jennifer coming onto the case, Mia tried focusing on the rest of the briefing while trying not to think about why Sean was not answering his phone.

As soon as the briefing was over, Mia wasted no time excusing herself and getting onto her phone and trying to call Sean again.

"Hello!"

Mia was surprised when a female answered Sean's phone after three rings and with an attitude.

Mia instantly caught one of her own. "Who the hell is this? Where is Sean?"

"Who the hell is this?" the woman spit back. "You called this phone looking for my fucking nephew!"

"Nephew?"

"That's what the fuck I just said! Now who the fuck is you?"

Mia felt really stupid now, so she introduced herself to the woman and then apologized for the way she spoke to her.

"Honey, it's fine," she told Mia. "I guess I owe you an apology as well because things are really messed up right now, and Sean just got arrested for punching out a police officer, child."

"He what?" Mia yelled in disbelief at what the hell she just heard her boyfriend's auntie just tell her. "This has to be a damn joke, right?"

"Baby, does it sound like I'm playing? We're all down at the county jail right now trying to find out what the hell is going on."

"I'm on my way there right now!" Mia told the woman, already rushing back into the office to collect her things to get the hell out of there.

ELEVEN

Mia arrived at the county jail ten minutes after rushing out of the briefing she had just ended with her boss. Mia and Jennifer ran across the parking lot and rushed straight into the front lobby to see three women and two guys crowded inside. Mia remembered the Latino female from their first meeting back at Sean's condo.

"Nina, right?" Mia asked as respectfully and nicely as she could. "I'm Mia."

"I know who the hell you are," Nina stated with attitude, looking Mia over yet unwilling to admit that the woman was actually very attractive.

"You the woman I just spoke to over the phone?" Toni asked, standing up from where she was seated beside Marvin. "I'm Toni. Sean's my nephew."

Mia shook the woman's hand and introduced Jennifer.

"What's happened with Sean? Why did he attack a police officer?" she asked.

"Because his fucking cousin was locked up while his ass was probably laying with your ass somewhere!" Nina spit at Mia nastily.

"Nina, chill!" Hulk spoke up as he walked over to stand beside her. "We're not here for that! We all trying to get Tony, T.J., and Sean outta this shit!"

"Honey, I'm really not all too sure what my nephew is doing," Toni explained to Mia. "But the last thing he told me was that he would be seeing me later, so now I'm waiting!"

Mia was unsure of what was really going on, so she

turned to Jennifer to say something just as the front door swung open. First the chief of police in full uniform walked into the lobby, followed by another guy dressed in a navy-blue suit.

"What the hell?" Jennifer said, sliding up beside Mia as they stood watching the chief of police and company walk up to the front desk, surprising them all when he demanded to know what Antonio Carter and Travis Johnson were being investigated for.

~ ~ ~

Mia was more unsure of what was really going on now than when she first arrived at the jail. She and Jennifer sat talking with Sean's family after both the chief and his associate walked from the front door to the back of the jail. She was trying to understand it all, after learning of the shooting of Sean's friend and cousin, just as she heard Sean's name called out.

She looked up to see Sean and two other young men she did not recognize being escorted through the jail out front where she and the others were waiting. Mia stood from her seat to greet her man, only for Nina to rush in front of her to get to Sean first, throw her arms around his neck, and kiss him directly on the lips.

Mia controlled herself from snatching the young Latin bitch off of Sean, but she did not want to have a showdown at the jail. Instead, Mia walked over to the chief of police and asked, "Sir, may I speak with you a moment?"

"What can I do for you, young lady?" Chief Smith asked, smiling at the gorgeous young woman.

Mia introduced herself as Special Agent Mia

Washington and explained her relationship with Sean, saying he was her fiancé. Mia then questioned the chief on the charges brought up against Sean, Tony, and T.J.

"Not to worry, Agent Washington," the chief said to Mia with a smile. "All charges against Mr. Antonio Carter, Mr. Travis Jackson, and Mr. Sean Carter have been dropped."

"Can you tell me—?"

"Sean!"

Once she heard his name called out, Mia swung her head around to see him walking out the door. She quickly thanked the chief before rushing after Sean and seeing him jog across the street and head toward the parking lot.

~ ~ ~

Sean used the key remote and unlocked Nina's

Charger as he jogged up to the car. He then snatched open the driver's door and had just climbed into the car, only for the passenger door to swing open and Mia hop inside.

"What are you doing, Mia?" Sean calmly asked her before closing the door.

"That's exactly what I was going to ask you!" she responded, staring dead into his eyes that seemed as if they were glowing. "What's going on, Sean? Where are you going?"

"Mia, I don't have time to explain now," he told her after shutting the car door.

"Well, then tell me on the way to wherever we're going," she told him, shutting the passenger door and putting on her seatbelt.

Sean stared at Mia a few moments and could see

she was dead serious. He did not bother arguing any further as he simply started up the Charger and in moments he had the sports car flying away from the county jail.

~ ~ ~

"Sean, where are we going?" Mia asked him after riding in complete silence for the past ten minutes with only the sound of the car's engine screaming as Sean pushed the Charger to almost 90 mph.

"Mia, I need to handle something," he calmly told her.

Mia waited a few minutes for Sean to say more, but after realizing he was not going to offer anything, she said, "Sean, you plan on telling me what's going on or not?"

"It's better if you don't know, Mia!"

"Excuse me!" Mia yelled. "Hell no, Sean! You're going to tell me something, and I mean now!"

Sean turned his head in Mia's direction and looked into her pissed-off eyes. He then focused back on the road as he said, "I'm going to find out who put the hit out on my cousin, Mia. I've got an idea, but I still gotta deal with another problem as well."

Still staring at Sean, Mia sighed after a moment and then said, "You're going to kill whoever it was who shot up your cousin and friend, aren't you, Sean?"

"I am after I get the answer to my question first!" Sean admitted to her.

Mia turned her head and stared out the window after hearing her boyfriend admit to planning a murder. Mia sat a few moments in thought before she finally said, "Okay!"

Sean heard Mia and looked back over at her. He said nothing more, but he fully understood what Mia's okay really meant.

~ ~ ~

"Which house is it?" Mia asked as Sean turned the Charger down the street on which he had explained the target lived.

"That's it right there!" Sean stated, just as he stopped the Charger directly in front of the house, only to climb quickly from the car to the sound of Mia calling out to him.

"Park the car!" Sean yelled back as he entered the front gate of the same house that was described to him back at the jail.

Sean walked up to the front porch and heard a television on inside. He kicked in the door, sending it flying open as he stepped inside the house to the screams of two females who were seated in the front room.

"Where the hell is—?" Sean called out, but paused to look over at the flat-screen that was playing loudly. He forcefully pushed the flat-screen from the wall it hung from, sending it crashing down to the floor. He then turned his attention back to the two women and continued what he was saying, "Where's Menace at?"

"He's not here!" one of the two girls answered in a shaky voice as she stared up fearfully at Sean.

"Where is he?" Sean asked just as he heard someone enter the house.

He looked back over his shoulder to see Mia step inside.

He turned back to the two women and continued

with his questioning, only to find out that Menace did not live at the house. But he did come by every other day or two to see Kim, who was his girlfriend and owner of the house. Sean gave a small smirk when Kim admitted that Menace did just call and say that he was on his way over to bring her something.

Sean turned to Mia and told her to stay with the two women as he started for the front door, only to hear Mia call out and ask, "Where are you going now?"

"To wait outside for Menace!" Sean answered as he stepped outside onto the front porch.

~ ~ ~

Menace pulled up to his lady's house after picking up a little something to eat for her and her sister, who was supposedly spending the night. He parked his Impala and then grabbed the bags that held the rib dinner inside. He climbed from his car and was just locking it up when he looked up and froze at the sight of Kim's front door that had been kicked open.

"What the fuck!" Menace said.

He dropped the food as he took off running while pulling out his .45 from under his shirt. He rushed into the front yard and up onto the porch, yelling out for Kim as he shot through the front door.

"Baby!" Kim cried out from beside her sister.

"What the fuck happened?" Menace asked with anger lacing his voice. He started toward Kim when he heard the all-too-familiar sound of a gun being cocked, which drew his attention to his left to look down the front end of a Glock.

"Drop your weapon and get on your knees, and then put your hands on top of your head!" Mia demanded as she held her Glock 17 trained onto Menace's head.

"Who the fuck is you?" Menace asked with a growl, ignoring the demand as he turned to face the stupid-as-hell female that was pointing a gun at him. "Bitch, if you don't get that—!"

He never got the rest of his words out as pain exploded from the left side of his face, sending him fast and hard to the ground. Glass could be heard shattering all around him. He felt someone help him to sit up as he shook his head as clear as he could, only to look up and see a guy dressed in black jeans, a black wifebeater, and brown Timberlands standing over him.

"Who the fuck is you?"

"The one you should be calling crazy!" Sean answered, before kicking Menace in the face and knocking his ass back down and out cold.

~ ~ ~

Sean grew tired of waiting after the girls tried shaking Menace and even lightly slapping him. Sean walked over to where Menace was laid across the sofa and slapped him hard across the face with the .45 that belonged to Menace.

"What the fuck!" Menace jerked up right out of his sleep after being slapped across the face. He paused and sat frozen after quickly noticing the guy with the gun aimed directly at him. "Who you supposed to be? Why you here?"

"Tony Carter!" Sean said. "You know the name?"

"Naw!" Menace answered, and was immediately back-handed across the face with his own .45 by the guy in front of him.

"Let's try this again!" Sean told him, aiming the .45 at Menace's left knee. "I'ma ask you this question again, and this time if you lie to me, I'm first destroying your left knee and then your right, and we'll just work our way upward after that. Do you know Tony Carter?"

"Fuck no!"

Boom!

"Aaaaaahhhhhhh!" Menace screamed in pain after his knee was blown off.

Sean ignored the hollering and attempted to ask his question again. But he had to pause a few moments from all the yelling and screaming Menace was doing. He slapped Menace across the face again, shutting the boy up and then asking his question again, "Tony Carter. Do you know him?"

"Man, fuck!"

Boom!

Sean blew out Menace's right knee as he promised he would. He then shifted his aim toward the boy's stomach when Mia got in the way, grabbing his arm and pulling him away from his target.

"Sean, what the hell is wrong with you?" Mia asked with anger easily heard in her voice. "What are you trying to do? If you're going to question him and want answers, then find a better way to get them, because your way isn't fucking working!"

"You're right," Sean said, slowly nodding his head.

Sean walked back over to where Menace was bleeding and crying out in pain.

"All right, we're going to try this a little differently this time. I'm going to ask you a question, and if you lie or I think you're lying to me, I'm gonna kill your girlfriend."

Aiming the .45 at Kim, Sean asked, "Do you know Tony Carter?"

"Yeah, man! Yeah, I know the muthafucker. Now just stop aiming that shit at my fucking girl!"

Sean slowly smiled and shifted his eyes to look over at Mia, who stood up staring angrily at him. He then winked his eye at her and got her to shake her head and roll her eyes back at him as a reward.

~ ~ ~

After getting the information out of Menace that he wanted, Sean drove the Charger in complete silence and deep thought, putting things together on how he was going to get back at everyone responsible for the attempt on his cousin and T.J. He lost his train of thought when he heard Mia call out his name.

"Yeah, Mia!" he answered, looking from the road over to her.

"Where are we going now?"

"I'm taking you home!" he explained, but then added, "I got a few things to handle."

"You're going after the guy Menace told you about, aren't you?"

Sean looked over his back at Mia.

"Some things I'd rather you don't know, Mia. I trust you, but I don't want to put you in a bad situation where both me and your job are put to the test and you have to decide where your loyalty is."

"You think I wouldn't choose you, don't you, Sean?" Mia questioned him, seeing the look he gave her before focusing back on the road.

After getting Mia back to her apartment, Sean shook his head when she angrily hopped out of the car and stormed off into the lobby of their building. Sean sighed deeply as he pulled off and headed back out to handle unfinished business.

To be continued . . .

To order books, please fill out the order form below:
To order films please go to www.good2gofilms.com

Name: _____

Address:_____

City: _____ State: _____ Zip Code: _____

Phone:_____

Email:_____

Method of Payment: Check   VISA   MASTERCARD

Credit Card#:_ _____

Name as it appears on card: _____

Signature: _____

Item Name	Price	Qty	Amount
48 Hours to Die – Silk White	$14.99		
A Hustler's Dream - Ernest Morris	$14.99		
A Hustler's Dream 2 - Ernest Morris	$14.99		
A Thug's Devotion – J. L. Rose and J. M. McMillon	$14.99		
All Eyes on Tommy Gunz – Warren Holloway	$14.99		
Black Reign – Ernest Morris	$14.99		
Bloody Mayhem Down South – Trayvon Jackson	$14.99		
Bloody Mayhem Down South 2 – Trayvon Jackson	$14.99		
Business Is Business – Silk White	$14.99		
Business Is Business 2 – Silk White	$14.99		
Business Is Business 3 – Silk White	$14.99		
Cash In Cash Out – Assa Raymond Baker	$14.99		
Cash In Cash Out 2 - Assa Raymond Baker	$14.99		
Childhood Sweethearts – Jacob Spears	$14.99		
Childhood Sweethearts 2 – Jacob Spears	$14.99		
Childhood Sweethearts 3 - Jacob Spears	$14.99		
Childhood Sweethearts 4 - Jacob Spears	$14.99		
Connected To The Plug – Dwan Marquis Williams	$14.99		
Connected To The Plug 2 – Dwan Marquis Williams	$14.99		
Connected To The Plug 3 – Dwan Williams	$14.99		
Deadly Reunion – Ernest Morris	$14.99		
Dream's Life – Assa Raymond Baker	$14.99		

Flipping Numbers – Ernest Morris	$14.99		
Flipping Numbers 2 – Ernest Morris	$14.99		
He Loves Me, He Loves You Not - Mychea	$14.99		
He Loves Me, He Loves You Not 2 - Mychea	$14.99		
He Loves Me, He Loves You Not 3 - Mychea	$14.99		
He Loves Me, He Loves You Not 4 – Mychea	$14.99		
He Loves Me, He Loves You Not 5 – Mychea	$14.99		
Kings of the Block – Dwan Willams	$14.99		
Kings of the Block 2 – Dwan Willams	$14.99		
Lord of My Land – Jay Morrison	$14.99		
Lost and Turned Out – Ernest Morris	$14.99		
Love Hates Violence – De'Wayne Maris	$14.99		
Love Hates Violence 2 – De'Wayne Maris	$14.99		
Love Hates Violence 3 – De'Wayne Maris	$14.99		
Love Hates Violence 4 – De'Wayne Maris	$14.99		
Married To Da Streets – Silk White	$14.99		
M.E.R.C. - Make Every Rep Count Health and Fitness	$14.99		
Mercenary In Love – J.L. Rose & J.L. Turner	$14.99		
Money Make Me Cum – Ernest Morris	$14.99		
My Besties – Asia Hill	$14.99		
My Besties 2 – Asia Hill	$14.99		
My Besties 3 – Asia Hill	$14.99		
My Besties 4 – Asia Hill	$14.99		
My Boyfriend's Wife - Mychea	$14.99		
My Boyfriend's Wife 2 – Mychea	$14.99		
My Brothers Envy – J. L. Rose	$14.99		
My Brothers Envy 2 – J. L. Rose	$14.99		
Naughty Housewives – Ernest Morris	$14.99		
Naughty Housewives 2 – Ernest Morris	$14.99		
Naughty Housewives 3 – Ernest Morris	$14.99		
Naughty Housewives 4 – Ernest Morris	$14.99		

Never Be The Same – Silk White	$14.99		
Shades of Revenge – Assa Raymond Baker	$14.99		
Slumped – Jason Brent	$14.99		
Someone's Gonna Get It – Mychea	$14.99		
Stranded – Silk White	$14.99		
Supreme & Justice – Ernest Morris	$14.99		
Supreme & Justice 2 – Ernest Morris	$14.99		
Supreme & Justice 3 – Ernest Morris	$14.99		
Tears of a Hustler - Silk White	$14.99		
Tears of a Hustler 2 - Silk White	$14.99		
Tears of a Hustler 3 - Silk White	$14.99		
Tears of a Hustler 4- Silk White	$14.99		
Tears of a Hustler 5 – Silk White	$14.99		
Tears of a Hustler 6 – Silk White	$14.99		
The Last Love Letter – Warren Holloway	$14.99		
The Last Love Letter 2 – Warren Holloway	$14.99		
The Panty Ripper - Reality Way	$14.99		
The Panty Ripper 3 – Reality Way	$14.99		
The Solution – Jay Morrison	$14.99		
The Teflon Queen – Silk White	$14.99		
The Teflon Queen 2 – Silk White	$14.99		
The Teflon Queen 3 – Silk White	$14.99		
The Teflon Queen 4 – Silk White	$14.99		
The Teflon Queen 5 – Silk White	$14.99		
The Teflon Queen 6 - Silk White	$14.99		
The Vacation – Silk White	$14.99		
Tied To A Boss - J.L. Rose	$14.99		
Tied To A Boss 2 - J.L. Rose	$14.99		
Tied To A Boss 3 - J.L. Rose	$14.99		
Tied To A Boss 4 - J.L. Rose	$14.99		
Tied To A Boss 5 - J.L. Rose	$14.99		

Time Is Money - Silk White	$14.99		
Tomorrow's Not Promised – Robert Torres	$14.99		
Tomorrow's Not Promised 2 – Robert Torres	$14.99		
Two Mask One Heart – Jacob Spears and Trayvon Jackson	$14.99		
Two Mask One Heart 2 – Jacob Spears and Trayvon Jackson	$14.99		
Two Mask One Heart 3 – Jacob Spears and Trayvon Jackson	$14.99		
Wrong Place Wrong Time – Silk White	$14.99		
Young Goonz – Reality Way	$14.99		
Subtotal:			
Tax:			
Shipping (Free) U.S. Media Mail:			
Total:			

Make Checks Payable To:
Good2Go Publishing
7311 W Glass Lane,
Laveen, AZ 85339

CPSIA information can be obtained
at www.ICGtesting.com
Printed in the USA
LVHW020727280220
648380LV00017B/332